AF612156

My Books

Fiction

- *Shards of Glass*

Non Fiction

- *How to Live with Bipolar*
- *Bipolar 1 Disorder Rescue Plan*
- *37 Symptoms of Bipolar Depression*
- *The Bipolar Guide*
- *A Practical Guide to Overcoming Loneliness*

Poetry

- *We Never Did Mornings*

BOOK 1

DOROTHY ALTER

SHARDS OF GLASS

CHAPTER 1

Cannes, France

"For better or for worse..." I really should have thought that through before getting involved with Louise. But at forty-two, for some reason that seemed plausible at the time, I lost all control of my senses and fell hopelessly in love with her.

I met Louise, quite by chance, at my friend Jean-Claude's new house overlooking the beach. There she was, the sunlight catching her hair, sitting on the couch, reading something on her Kindle.

"Richard, this is Louise," Jean-Claude said.

Suddenly, she jumped up and looked at her watch. "Oh, I'm late for an appointment. I really must go."

When she came towards me, I shook her warm hand and breathed in her perfume. It smelled like a mixture of vanilla and citrus and made my head spin.

"We must meet again when I don't have to dash off," she said.

I am a tall man, over six feet, and it surprised me to see Louise, in her high-heeled shoes, was almost as tall as me. Her striking appearance was heart-stopping.

“See you again, then,” I said. My face dropped with disappointment that she was going so soon, and I hoped she didn’t notice.

“Are you dating her?” I asked Jean-Claude.

“Oh, no,” he said, laughing. “She’s my cousin.”

I took a deep breath and smiled. “I didn’t know you had a cousin in Cannes.”

“She doesn’t live here. She lives in Paris.” Then he looked me in the eye and said, “Don’t get too involved with Louise. I love her, but she is big trouble.” His comment intrigued me, but I thought nothing more of it.

CHAPTER 2

The next day, I was sitting in my sunny living room reading a book, the flimsy curtain blowing through the open window, when the phone rang. It was Louise. At the sound of her voice, my ears pricked up and my heart beat harder in my chest.

"Would you like to go to see *'Pierrot le Fou'* at the *Cinema Olympia* on Thursday?" she asked. "A friend of Jean-Claude gave me a couple of tickets."

I closed my book and put it down on the table. "Yes," I said, smiling to myself. "We can get dinner afterwards. Where can I pick you up?"

"I'll meet you at the theater at seven o'clock," she said and hung up.

She was certainly not shy about asking a man for a date, even a man she had only just met. I was definitely interested in Louise and wanted to get to know her, but being a bit of a hermit, I rarely dated women, preferring to stay at home with a good book. But Louise was different. The thought of her sent shivers up my spine. I looked forward to seeing her again.

CHAPTER 3

On Thursday evening, I was standing outside the *Cinema Olympia* on time, a noisy line of people at the ticket booth behind me. They were mainly couples in their twenties and thirties, and there were a few families with children laughing and chatting. It was summer, so most people dressed casually, some in shorts and flip-flops, as they had probably just come back from the beach. Most of them were speaking French, of course, but I had been in France for several years now so could understand what they said.

I looked at my watch – five minutes past seven, but there was no sign of Louise. Beginning to wonder if she had changed her mind, my hands shook at the thought of being stood up. I gave her another ten minutes, then stamped my foot. Why was I standing there waiting for her like a fool?

I looked around and saw that all the people had gone while I was waiting outside the cinema. I swore under my breath when I realized she really had stood me up. If this was what she was like, then I didn't want to know her after all. I looked over at the car park. No Louise. There was nothing else for it but to go home and find something else to do for the evening. I strode over to my car, unlocked the door, and went home. One thing was for sure, I would never speak to her again.

CHAPTER 4

Arlette came to greet me at the door, and I nearly tripped over her. She rubbed up against my leg, purring, and I gave her a couple of treats from the jar I kept by the front door. They were tuna-flavored and smelled awful, but she swallowed them whole. "Hello, my little friend," I said, and she meowed in reply. Then she followed me into the kitchen, bushy, white tail in the air. I made myself a large pot of coffee, then I put on some music, 'Bohemian Rhapsody.' It was just the way I was feeling. I plopped into my favorite chair in the living room, lit a cigar, and took a draw. The earthy smell of cigars always made me feel relaxed. I settled back into my leather armchair with the book I was reading about the Gothic architecture in Prague.

Taking a sip of my coffee, I nearly jumped out of my chair because it felt like fire on my tongue. I gritted my teeth in a sudden fit of anger when I thought of Louise. What had I done to deserve such terrible treatment? I turned the whole thing over and over in my mind. Perhaps she didn't like me after all. Perhaps she had made the date because she felt sorry for me. I took another draw on my cigar and watched the smoke ring form in the air.

Jean-Claude would be most embarrassed if he knew what she'd done. I felt sure of that. And what about our dinner date after the film? I scoffed. Now I would have to hunt around for something to eat. I took another sip of my coffee and turned the page in my book. I wouldn't even bother thinking about her, let alone calling to see what was wrong.

Then the phone rang.

"Richard?" It was Louise.

"Yes," I said in a clipped tone of voice.

The phone went dead for a moment.

"I'm terribly sorry. I was busy and got carried away. I completely forgot I was going to meet you at the cinema tonight."

I scoffed. Why had she made a date then forgotten all about it? The phone felt weighty in my hand, and I thought I should probably hang up. But she was Jean-Claude's cousin, so I listened to what she had to say.

"Let me take you out to dinner tomorrow," she said, "by way of an apology."

I tapped my fingers on the phone and considered it. Did I really want to go out to dinner with a woman who thought nothing of standing me up? Was I ridiculous, or what? But I had that nagging feeling that maybe she really had forgotten, and I should be more forgiving.

I switched the phone to the other ear. “Where would you like to go?”

“I thought we could try one of the little restaurants in *Quartier des Anglais*. Can you pick me up at Jean-Claude’s house tomorrow night at eight?”

Much to my surprise, I said ‘yes.’

CHAPTER 5

The next night, I drove round to Jean-Claude's new house at eight o'clock to pick up Louise. She wasn't ready, so I had to wait. Jean-Claude was in the living room unpacking from the move. A tall, lanky guy, I thought he looked comical, squatting on the floor with his legs tucked underneath him. He pushed his square glasses up on his nose. "Women are always late," he said. "You have to allow them time to get ready."

"Yes, but it is annoying," I said.

I knelt beside him and held open a box while he took out some books and put them on the floor. They looked like new books, shiny in their dust jackets. Maybe he had meant to read them and hadn't got around to it yet. He leaned in towards me and said in a hushed tone, "You've had one failed marriage to Colette, remember? I wouldn't risk getting too involved with Louise."

Yes, my marriage to Colette had been a disaster, I thought. We were totally incompatible. She liked to go out and mix with people, whereas I am a home body. I rememebered the times she would drag me out to some party or the other, often without invitation, and she would be the center of attetion. She would be laughing and telling jokes with her friends, and when she had had enough Champagne, her laughter could be heard rising higher and higher in the room. I used to shrink back in a corner and wish we could go home.

I frowned. "Aren't you going to tell me what Louise has done?" I said and laughed nervously. "You make her sound terrible."

Jean-Claude sat back and looked at me. His mouth formed a tight line. "I'm just saying you're playing with fire, that's all."

I thrust my fists deep into the pockets of my jacket. Should I cancel Louise's dinner plans and make up some excuse, or should I go ahead anyway and ignore Jean-Claude and his advice? I had the distinct feeling that my life would change forever if I got to know Louise. I just didn't realize how much.

Just then, she appeared in the doorway. She looked magnificent in her tight white dress and pink high-heeled shoes. She had the kind of skin that reminded me of an alabaster doll. I thought it must be quite a challenge for her to keep out of the sun in Cannes.

"Hi," I said. "You look lovely." My voice wavered slightly. Perhaps I should tell her I felt sick, and we had to call it off.

Then I changed my mind. "Let's go," I said, getting up from the floor. Jean-Claude frowned, and I wondered if I had done the right thing.

CHAPTER 6

We drove down to *Quartier des Anglais* and Louise pointed out a little hole-in-the-wall restaurant she said someone had recommended to her. All the spaces were full, so I had to park down the street. I squeezed out of the tight space and took her hand. After what Jean-Claude had said, it surprised me I didn't get an electric shock. I grinned to myself at the thought.

It was a popular time to eat in Cannes, so the restaurant was crowded. When we stepped inside, it was loud with chatter and laughter. We stood in the doorway and waited our turn to be seated. Then the *maitre d'* showed us to a table by the window where we could watch the passers-by on *Quartier des Anglais*.

The restaurant was small and dark, with a low ceiling. A glass lamp, with a flickering flame, glowed orange on our table. Louise smiled at me, and I thought she looked lovely.

A waiter came up to the table and gave us both a menu. "What can I get you to drink?"

Louise spread her napkin on her lap. "We'll have a bottle of

Beaujolais," she said. I let her choose the wine as she said she would pay the bill, but it embarrassed me none-the-less.

The waiter scuttled away to get the wine, and I looked at the menu. It was mostly seafood, which I really enjoyed, but there were also some steak dishes that sounded mouth-watering.

"I'll have the crab," Louise said when the waiter returned.

"The *steak au poivre*, for me."

Louise glanced at me and smiled. I placed my hand on hers on the table, then said, "How beautiful you look tonight." She smiled again.

I looked around to see if I knew anybody. The tourists stood out by a mile with their drastic tans and backpacks slung over the backs of their chairs. I breathed in the delicious smell of seafood and garlic, and it reminded me of a time when I'd had fresh lobster cooked right there at my table on the beach in Tenerife.

The meal was delicious. I gazed intently at Louise while she was eating, not because she looked lovely so much as to gauge whether Jean-Claude could possibly be right about her.

"Tell me about your home in Paris," I said.

She laughed. "Oh, I've lived there practically all my life. You must come up and see me sometime."

Well, that was an invitation if ever I heard one. Sadly, I was not fond of Paris, and I don't like flying, but thought I would definitely drive up there if she was to invite me.

"Have you been married before?" she asked.

"Yes, I was married for seven years," I said. "but I'm now a gay bachelor since the divorce."

"What did your wife do?"

"She was in the shoe business, not selling them, designing them. She was a very talented lady and quite well-known nationally. Although we wanted children, we never had any."

Louise suddenly said she needed to go to the restroom. She got up and practically ran away from the table. I reached out and touched her arm as she left. It looked as if she was going to throw up and I wondered if there was something wrong with her seafood.

I waited and waited. Time crept by, but Louise didn't come out of the restroom. Checking my watch, I realized she had been gone for at least ten minutes. I glanced at the other guests, not sure what I should do. Then I decided I would get another woman to go into the restroom and see what had happened to her. I quickly made my way across the room and caught one of the waitresses just as she was serving a meal to a group of four people.

I let her finish serving, then attracted her attention.

"Would you mind going into the restroom to see what's happened to my girlfriend, Louise?"

Moments later, Louise came back to the table.

"Are you alright?" I asked. She looked ashen, and I thought I should get her home as quickly as possible.

"Oh, yes, it was just a bit of anxiety," she said.

Louise paid for the meal like she said she would, and I felt my face flush with embarrassment when she put her credit card on the table. I said nothing more about her anxiety, but it worried me, nonetheless.

CHAPTER 7

We saw each other almost every day for the next week and had elaborate dinners in all the places where the rich and famous were to be seen. Then we walked hand in hand along the cobbled streets, stopping at the market stalls and the little cafes where all the fashionable people met. We went to every movie in town and indulged in cocktails for two afterwards. And we drove around the countryside in my vintage BMW, stopping at glamorous spas for massages and pedicures along the way.

Once, we stopped at a little country inn with sawdust floors, and beams so low I had to duck my head when we walked in. It reminded me of the pubs in Kent in England where I was born. I wondered, sometimes, if I missed Kent, but I had been in France for so long now, Kent no longer seemed like home. I don't know what attracted me to France, exactly, but I loved it here and couldn't think of ever leaving. Of course, my sister Amy wanted me to be nearer to her, especially now that Frank had died, but nothing is as cut and dried as that. I visited her quite often, and that had to suffice.

Louise and I shared a meal of clams in a rich sauce, and the garlicky smell and taste were amazing. While we were eating, we both drank tankards of ale. She smiled at me, and I looked into her deep brown eyes. They were fathomless, and I had no idea what she was thinking.

Louise was one of those women who could wear any color and still look great. That day, she had on a red blouse with some buttons undone at the front. Her ample breasts pushed up against the cloth. I looked at her and got the distinct impression that she liked to be seen in public. If she lived in Cannes, she would likely be a socialite like Colette and I would never be able to keep up with her. I wondered why I was so attracted to gregarious women, and couldn't think why they interested me so much.

"It's lovely to see you so happy," I said, and she squeezed my hand. Yet, there was still that niggling doubt that Jean-Claude had intimated about Louise. Was it about her anxiety? I didn't think so. It was like a worm in an apple. It wouldn't give me any peace until I found out what he meant.

On Tuesday afternoon, I took Louise to my favorite cafe down at the port. It felt like my second home, since I spent so much time there. It was strange that I hadn't taken her there before, seeing as I called in every morning for breakfast.

When we arrived, it surprised me how packed the cafe was. Usually, I am there at six in the morning before the tourists are out for the day. I like to have it to myself and wasn't used to the din. The coffee machine whirred and sputtered on the counter. Loud music played in the background, and I could hardly hear myself think above the noise.

We sat down at a little table by the window and looked out at the marina with all its enormous yachts only the rich and famous could afford. When the barista came, I said, "*Bonjour*, Michelle? We'd like two coffees, please." I glanced at Louise. "Would you like something to eat?"

"Some chocolate cake, please." So, Michelle brought it to the table for her.

Louise was still a mystery, so I leaned forward and asked her outright. "Tell me a little about yourself," I said, and waited expectantly.

She smiled. "Well, let's see. I'm thirty-eight. My marriage ended amicably, but we had no children, and I don't see him anymore."

So, she had been married before as well. Maybe she had a good divorce settlement. By the way she dressed, she certainly didn't seem hard up for cash. "What have you done since then?" I asked.

She was a little evasive, and I thought she wasn't going to tell me. Then she said, "I worked for a fashion magazine for some time." She didn't tell me what she did now. I waited, but she didn't say any more.

I looked around the cafe and spotted Mylan sitting on his own in the corner. We sometimes met for lunch in the old part of town, but I hadn't seen him for weeks. Mylan was gay, and I had known him and his partner Jacques for many years.

"I've just seen a friend," I said to Louise. "You don't mind if he joins us, do you?" I waved, and Mylan came over and sat down. He was a handsome guy with red hair and a beard, and he had a whole bevy of women friends.

As soon as he pulled out his seat, his face lit up. "Louise, how are you?" he said in his deep voice. "What a nice surprise."

Louise had a strange look on her face, as if Mylan was the last person she wanted to meet that day.

"Hello, Mylan," she said.

I looked from one to the other. "How do you two know each other?" I asked, perplexed. As far as I knew Louise had always lived in Paris, but perhaps I was wrong.

"We go way back," she said with a little, nervous laugh.

"You could say we grew up together when Louise lived in Cames," Mylan said. "I see her quite often when she comes down from Paris." He gestured with his hands. "We know the same people in town. We go to the same art exhibitions."

I had no idea that Louise would know Mylan. But judging by

her expression, she didn't seem to want to know him then.

Mylan looked intently at Louise. "How's your father?" he said, in a hushed tone of voice as if he didn't want to be heard above the din.

"He's well," she said and smiled. "Have you had a chance to see the show in town yet?"

"I'm going with Jacques on Saturday."

"I've recently added five new pieces of abstract art to my collection in Paris."

"I only wish I could see them," Mylan said.

I frowned. So, Louise had a father. Why hadn't she mentioned him to me? I assumed both her parents were dead like mine, but, of course, Louise was younger than me, so her parents were probably still alive. Where did her father live I wondered? I hardly joined in the conversation because I was wondering why Louise had been so quick to change the subject when Mylan mentioned her father. Why was she acting this way?

Strangely, we never made love in the whole week she was there. I did get her in a few compromising positions more than once, but she shied away. For some reason, this didn't bother me at all. I was certain we would have incredible sex if I was to keep seeing her.

It wasn't until the next day that I looked at all the receipts I had accumulated from money spent on Louise's visit. Then I panicked and realized she was a woman who would be very high maintenance. Now that I'd had this revelation, I vowed never to touch my investments or my inheritance to cater to Louise's expensive tastes. I am a wealthy man on paper, but I wasn't going to get caught out by a gold-digger. I wondered again, where her money came from. She didn't seem to work any more, so perhaps it came from her divorce. I would find out sooner or later.

CHAPTER 8

Then Louise went away. It seemed quite sudden, although she'd told me the first day I met her that she would be going back to Paris soon. I felt my heart would burst when I put her into a taxi and waved goodbye.

The next day, I sat in my kitchen and toyed with the phone. Should I call her, or not? Should I ask if she got back safely to Paris? I checked my texts again. Nothing from her. So maybe that's what Jean-Claude meant when he said she was unreliable. Should I be the one to text her, maybe? We'd had a wonderful week together and I wanted to see her again. I took a draw of my cigar and rested it in the ashtray. Then I thought about her visit and gasped. Surely, Louise hadn't used me for my money. Had she bled me dry, then disappeared?

I wandered about in a daze for the next two weeks, calling and calling, but all my messages went through to voice mail. I texted her several times, but the same thing happened. Should I be sensible and put it down to a temporary fling? But that didn't seem to satisfy me. I just had to see her again.

Although Jean-Claude warned me about Louise, I thought it

was possible I was falling in love with her. I wanted to see her, and I didn't want to wait. Then I decided, on the spur of the moment, to visit Paris and see what had become of her. Jean-Claude gave me her address because I told him I had to send her a parcel. I hoped she wouldn't be mad at me if I turned up out of the blue. My neighbor said he would look after Arlette.

CHAPTER 9

Paris, France

Before I could change my mind, I hurriedly packed a carry-on bag and made sure I included my favorite shirt. I wondered, absently, if I might get to stay at Louise's apartment, or was that wishful thinking? As an afterthought, I put a book I was reading into my bag, just in case I had to stay in a hotel. Of course, it would be easier to fly, but I preferred to drive.

I got into my BMW, put the carry-on bag on the back seat, and started my journey up north. My car hadn't been outside of Cannes in six months, and I wasn't sure how it would fair on the *autoroute* to Paris. It was a classic BMW, but I prayed it would be reliable. Then, just outside Paris, I heard a clunking noise, and the car broke down. I swore, got out of the car, and looked underneath. Of course, it was too low to the ground so I couldn't see a thing.

I dialed a number on my phone. "My car's broken down on the *autoroute*," I said. It's just south of Paris, just before you get to the city. A dark blue BMW."

They arrived in no time and towed me to the nearest garage. One of the mechanics, a bald guy with a dark mustache, walked around my car and whistled through his teeth. "Not bad at all," he said with a grin, and I felt a rush of pride in my chest.

I finally got to the city and reached into my pocket to find Louise's address:125 *Place de la Mairie*. My GPS was working admirably, so I nudged the vehicle into an empty space outside the block of apartment buildings where she lived. I looked across the street and saw the tall, gray building with glazed tiles and wrought-iron railings. There were steps leading up to an archway where someone could stand if it was raining. It was a very grand building, and I could well see Louise living there. I totted up how much it might cost to rent an apartment on this side of town and my heart nearly stopped. Was Louise a woman of means, or did she have someone else to pay her bills? I vowed it wouldn't be me.

I had to squeeze out of the car because the spaces were so close together in her street. Then I strode across the sidewalk and up the steep steps to the front door.

Standing on the doorstep, I broke out in a cold sweat. The whole situation was ridiculous. Why did I expect to turn up unannounced like this and not cause a scene? Louise probably had other things to do and didn't need me to interrupt her. My hands shook and I could barely breathe. But I knew I had come a long way to see her, so see her I would.

After some time, gathering my nerves, I found the number of her apartment on the bronze plate and rang the bell. The chime was the only sound to be heard in the street. It seemed so loud I was shocked it didn't cause all the neighbors to come running out of their apartments to take a look. I grinned to myself at the thought. But of course, it wasn't loud at all. If Louise was in, she would be the only one to hear it.

I waited, my knees feeling weak and sweat now forming on my forehead, but nothing happened. I rang again. Nothing. No Louise. I panicked. What if she had looked out of her window and seen me standing on the step? What if she didn't want to see me? Or what if she was away, and I had come all that way for nothing? I sighed and glanced up the street. A woman with a baby in an old stroller with filigree wheels passed by, but otherwise the street was empty. I decided that if Louise wasn't going to answer, I would stay in a hotel for the night and see if I could get hold of her in the morning.

I went to a hotel on the outskirts of Paris as I thought it would be cheaper than in the city, but I was wrong. It was very expensive indeed. Never mind. I hardly ever stayed in a hotel, so I could afford to splurge now and then.

CHAPTER 10

I had a substantial breakfast of bacon, eggs and a croissant and left the hotel at around 9 o'clock the next morning. I timed it like that because I thought Louise might like to lounge about in the mornings. Also, I was afraid of waking her if I called too early. I dressed in my favorite blue shirt, gathered up my carry-on bag, and walked outside to the car.

The traffic into Paris was horrendous; cars honking at each other, sirens blaring even though the morning rush hour was over. Maybe I should have left earlier, as it was after 10 o'clock when I arrived at her apartment.

I parked the car and walked up the steps to the front door. I rang the bell, then waited. Nobody answered. Biting my lip, I felt sweat forming in my armpits. This was not a good omen. Louise had probably gone out again, and I had missed her. Why didn't I leave the hotel sooner? Hoping she would open the door, or even come down to meet me, I rang the bell again. But no such luck. Louise was not going to answer. I sighed and walked back to the car. How stupid I had been. It served me right that she wasn't in. I thumped my fist on the leather steering wheel. What could I do now?

Then I had an idea. I decided to write her a note if I could find some notepaper. Soon, I had the front of the car upside down, looking in every nook and cranny, but no paper and certainly no pen could be found. I fell back in my seat and sighed. But no, I wouldn't be defeated, I would go to the *pharmacie* across the street and buy some paper and a pen.

When I got back in the car, I balanced the piece of paper on a book. "Dear Louse, I was in town on business, so I thought I would see if you were in. I hope you don't mind." That should do it.

I went back to Louise's apartment and slid the note under the door. I put her name on it, of course, so that the other residents would know it was for her. Then, just as I was leaving, I rang the bell just one more time, and Louise answered. I gasped. I had only been out for a few minutes to buy the paper and pen, yet there she was at home.

"Who is it?" she asked.

"Richard." Then I added for good measure, "I was in town and thought I would see how you were getting along."

I broke out in a cold sweat at the thought she would think I was lying. I was lying, of course, but I didn't want her to know that.

"Can I come up?" I said when she didn't answer.

There was a pause, and I was sure she would say, "No," but the heavy, green door sprung open, and I stepped inside.

Louise's apartment was on the top floor, and there was no elevator like in so many of these old buildings. My legs ached as I climbed the stairs. One, two, three, four, then I finally reached the fifth floor where Louise lived. I lived on the ground floor, so I wasn't used to that many stairs, and by the time I got up to the top of her apartment building, I was ready to sit down. I vowed to go to the gym more often when I got home.

When Louise opened the door, she had a blank look on her face, and I wondered if I should have come at all. I leaned forward and kissed her on both cheeks. They felt cold.

"Come in, Richard," she said. "I can't stop for long, as I have an appointment in half an hour."

Well, that was a turnoff for a start, but I couldn't say anything because I had arrived without telling her I was coming. She looked as amazing as she had in Cannes, and my heart must have missed a beat because I felt quite faint. Louise wore an off-white dress with a tight-fitting skirt that rode up her thighs when she sat down. I merely glanced at her legs so she wouldn't think I was staring. They were so lovely a shiver went up my back. She wore her usual high-heeled shoes, this time in an interesting shade of lavender to match her necklace and earrings.

"I haven't heard from you at all," I blurted out, even though I had vowed not to mention why she hadn't answered my phone calls and texts. "I thought something had happened to you and wondered if you'd got home safely."

"Oh," she said with a sudden laugh. "I know I should have called you, but I have been so busy since my return. You have no idea!"

I certainly had no idea. "I thought we were getting along fine, but I suppose I was wrong about that."

I was fishing, of course, but when she didn't answer, I suddenly began to feel quite foolish that I had made the trip.

"Would you like a drink?" she said. "I have a superb Merlot that I opened only yesterday."

When I nodded, she quickly got up, went into the kitchen and got some wine off of the counter.

While she was busy pouring the wine, I looked around the room. It was palatial, with high ceilings and crown molding. Scalloped paneling graced one wall, and a ceiling fan whirred above my head. Her furniture was of the usual French design, very elegant, and the chintz-covered sofa I was sitting on was so plush I could have gone to sleep. The entire room smelled of flowers. I thought the apartment must have cost her a fortune and wondered, yet again, where she got the money.

She returned from the kitchen with two long-stemmed, crystal glasses glinting in her hand. It was a very smooth Merlot, a deep red color, and I admired her taste.

"I've been ill," she said when she sat down.

I was shocked as only five minutes ago she said she had been so busy. Which one was it — had she been ill, or had she been out all the time? She perplexed me to no end.

"Yes, I came down with a nasty bug that I just couldn't shake off," she said. "It gave me a terrible stomachache, and I had a fever for a couple of days. I really should have gone to the hospital."

"I'm so sorry to hear that," I said, but somehow didn't believe her at all. And if she thought she should have gone to the hospital, why didn't she go?

She took a sip of her wine and I wondered how she would make her appointment in the ten minutes that were left before she had to go out. But she seemed to have forgotten all about that now.

"Are you thinking of coming down to Cannes again?" I asked. I didn't expect her to say, "Yes," but thought I would give it a try.

"Yes!" she said, and I raised my eyebrows. "I told Jean-Claude I would come down and help him with the furnishings for his new house. He has some ideas of his own, of course, but he said he would like my opinion." She smiled mysteriously. "And you know there is nothing I like better than shopping."

I smiled to myself and could imagine poor Jean-Claude trying to keep up with her suggestions of furnishings for his house. But he was her cousin, so I guessed he knew what he was getting himself into. He never seemed like the kind of man who would ask for a woman's opinion about anything, though, but Louise wanted me to believe that he had.

I smiled awkwardly as we sat there sipping our wine. Surely, she would have shown some sign of being happy to see me, but she didn't. I thought maybe she had a boyfriend in Paris that she had failed to mention when she was spending all my money in Cannes. If that was the case, I really should back out. I didn't want to get into any entanglements with another man. And surely, he must be very rich if he was buying her all these expensive things.

She put her glass down on the table and said, "I really have to leave now, Richard. It is only a short drive, but I don't want to be late."

We said our goodbyes, and I walked her to her car, which was parked next to mine, outside the apartment building. I opened the door for her and waited for her to step in.

"It was nice seeing you again," I said, and she smiled in answer.

CHAPTER 11

My shoulders slumped when I drove around the city on the way to the *autoroute*. The meeting had been very formal, nothing like I had imagined. We never even kissed properly. Not that I thought she would throw her arms around me, but I certainly hoped she would be happy to see me. When she was in Cannes, we had got on so well; I wondered what had happened in between.

When she didn't return my messages, I should have taken that as a hint. Surely, this must be the cold shoulder. Or the cold cheek, I thought, chuckling to myself. Perhaps she wasn't interested in me at all. Should I have waited until I heard from her? Why had I been so impulsive? Maybe the trip wasn't one of my best ideas.

I was out of the city now, on the *autoroute* to Cannes. Some joker slipped in front of me, and it was all I could do to brake and miss him.

I contemplated what an infuriating kind of woman Louise was. She would annoy me to no end if I stuck around, but I was very attracted to her, and I thought that wouldn't matter. I imagined what she would be like in bed and took a deep breath. Would she be submissive, I wondered? I hardly thought so.

I tried to concentrate on the road because I knew if I wasn't careful, I would have an accident. But my thoughts kept straying back to Louise.

The whole thing had been a complete disaster. I thought she had invented the appointment so she could be out of the apartment before I made myself comfortable. It was then that I felt sorry for myself, and it left a bitter taste on my tongue. I had spent all that money, stayed in an expensive hotel, then she hadn't made me feel welcome.

I took my eyes off the road for a minute and had to swerve back into my lane. The autoroute was always busy. Cars whizzed by on either side of me. It wasn't like driving around the streets in Cannes. I had to keep my eyes glued to the road.

My thoughts went back to Louise again, and I had to ask myself why I would be the least bit interested in a woman that was always making things up. I thought she lied to me all the time, but didn't like to admit it to myself. Why hadn't she returned my phone calls for a start? Even if you don't want to see someone again, surely it would be only polite to call them back when they'd left a message. But apparently Louise thought differently. I was just sorry I had gone at all. She'd made a fool of me, or had I made a fool of myself? The problem was, I was besotted with her, and I couldn't deny it.

CHAPTER 12

Cannes, France

Two weeks passed, and I wondered when Louise would come to visit Jean-Claude again. I thought of asking him, but I didn't want to seem too keen on her as he probably knew she didn't take to me. It was a difficult situation. Jean-Claude was a decent type of man who was usually a straight talker, and I wondered why he had been so evasive about Louise. I spent a couple of days thinking about calling him, but couldn't decide.

Then the next day, I called and asked him if he had heard from his cousin.

"Oh, Louise," he said, laughing. "I haven't heard from her at all. She was coming down but hasn't made a date. She can be so infuriating."

I didn't want to admit to Jean-Claude that I had been to Paris to see her, so I let him think we had spoken on the phone instead. "She said she was coming down to help you choose furnishings for your house," I said, to see what he would say.

"At least, that's what she had me believe."

Jean-Claude laughed again. "Oh, no, she won't be telling me what to choose. I wouldn't think of letting her. Louise has very expensive tastes. I'm sure you've noticed."

Well! I was dumbfounded. Hadn't she told me in Paris she was coming down to help Jean-Claude choose furnishings for his house? I was sure that's what she said.

"You must be careful with Louise," Jean-Claude said. "She will tell you one thing and mean another. She is not to be relied upon at all."

"That's terrible," I said, feeling rather foolish. "I thought she was amazing."

"That's Louise," he said. "You either love her or leave her. There are no two ways about it."

"I rather fell for Louise when she was here," I blurted out, feeling my face flush. "We had some marvelous times together."

"You had better beware. She will try your patience with all her stories and her strange opinions. I love her dearly. She's my cousin, but I wouldn't advise you to get too fond of her."

So, that was it. Louise had a reputation. She was not to be trusted. My heart sank. Surely, now that I had that piece of information confirmed, I should just forget all about her, yet even then, I couldn't bring myself to give up on her. Surely, she was not as bad as Jean-Claude made out. If or when she came down again to Cannes, I would find out for myself.

CHAPTER 13

Two weeks passed and not a word from Louise. I phoned a couple of times, got redirected to her voicemail, and gave up. Instead of forgetting all about her, though, I found myself thinking about her all the time.

Feeling foolish, I moped about in my apartment and even went off my food. That was very unlike me as I liked to cook and usually ate very well. For a couple of weeks, I lived on eggs, ham sandwiches, and the occasional salad, but it was not very satisfying. I wondered if Louise liked to cook and thought how nice it would be to make some gourmet meals together. But even then, I knew that was ridiculous. Louise was probably a terrible cook and had no intention of sharing the kitchen with me.

Her indifference towards me was painful. I didn't think I deserved that. In fact, I was so frustrated I couldn't sleep. Night after night I got up and paced in my living room thinking I should forget all about her. But I knew it was impossible. Somehow or other, she had got inside my head, and I couldn't get her out.

I suddenly remembered I had a photo of her. Somebody had

offered to take a photo of us together when we were walking down the beach. I reached out and grabbed my phone. There we were, arm in arm together on the beach, laughing at something we'd said. I studied the photo for a while and realized that Louise was rather over-dressed for a walk on the beach. She was wearing a long, flowing pink skirt and a tight, revealing blouse in a beautiful shade of green. Only Louise could get away with such a sumptuous outfit.

Then I noticed she was carrying her shoes, the normal spiky, high-heel shoes she favored. They were a brilliant shade of red. What ridiculous shoes Louise wore. They were so impractical. But somehow, she could get away with it and she looked amazing in them. I noticed that without her shoes, Louise was quite a bit shorter than me.

CHAPTER 14

Another week passed, and I was still obsessed with Louise. I knew it was ridiculous; she had probably forgotten I existed by now, but I couldn't get her out of my mind. I wondered what she was doing in her elegant apartment in Paris. What did she do to pass the time? She never mentioned any hobbies or interests, and certainly didn't mention any kind of work. I sat at my computer and thought I would send her an email, but didn't have her address, so closed the program.

Then on Sunday, the phone rang. It was her.

"*Bonjour*, Richard," she said. "How are you? I haven't heard from you in a while."

Well, that was stupid for a start. "I didn't expect to hear from you, Louise," I said, rather curtly. "In fact, I thought you didn't see my messages. I have called you numerous times." My face flushed, and my heart was thumping so hard in my chest, I felt sure she could hear it on the other end of the phone.

But instead of defending herself, she completely ignored what I said. "I just thought I would let you know I shall be coming down to Cannes again next week to stay with my cousin. He wants me to help him choose some rugs and a dining table for his new house."

"That's marvelous," I said.

Well, what do you know? She was coming down to Cannes to see her cousin and help him pick out some furnishings. It was crazy! But never mind. If she was coming, I would love to see her again. I tried to picture what she was wearing at the other end of the phone. Would she be in a long robe that came down to her ankles? Imaging her lounging on the wonderfully soft chintz sofa in her living room left me short of breath.

"I'm in Dijon at the moment, visiting a friend," she said, shattering that picture in my mind. So, she wasn't lounging on her sofa at all. She was in Dijon, way south of Paris.

When she ended the call, I asked myself if I should have sounded so eager. Would she have noticed that in my voice? Then I decided I didn't care what she thought. I would get to see her again, and that's all that mattered. Elated, I whistled a little tune when I went into the kitchen to make myself a chicken sandwich.

CHAPTER 15

Louise arrived on Saturday afternoon. I was out but got her text. I read it over and over again. My Louise (is that how I thought of her now?) was staying at Jean-Claude's house and I was only a couple of miles away. I smiled when I realized I was getting excited to see her again, but it wasn't clear if she would give me the time of day. I wondered if I should make the first move or wait for her to contact me. Then later that evening, I called her.

"*Bonsoir*, Louise," I said, tentatively. "How are you? I hope we shall see each other again now that you are in Cannes. It's been a long time since my visit to Paris and I've wondered how you've been." Was I talking too much? Was I boring her, maybe?

"I thought we might go out tonight," she said, quite unexpectedly. I knew she was a forward woman, but I still wasn't used to women initiating dates. "I've missed going for drives in the countryside. It's so stuffy in Cannes this time of year, the tourists are swarming like flies all over the place."

I raised my eyebrows. I certainly wanted to go for a drive that evening with Louise and was so pleased she had suggested it.

"That sounds wonderful. Would you like to eat somewhere nice before we go?"

"Oh, that's so sweet of you, Richard, but Jean-Claude is having a barbecue. He's cooking steak."

A barbecue with steak! I would dearly love to eat that, but I wasn't invited. I tensed up. Why had she even told me about it if she wasn't going to invite me to join them? Louise was a very difficult woman to fathom. She was unlike anyone I had ever known.

"Well, I'll pick you up at 8 o'clock then."

After a tasteless salad in my apartment, I washed the BMW, polished the headlamps, and put the hood down. Even though the car was old, the dark blue paintwork shone like glass, and I was very proud of her.

I wondered what had happened between Louise and me. We were practically lovers the last time she was in Cannes, yet in Paris we were like strangers. It was odd. I felt like a fool, but I would accept it if that was the way Louise wanted to proceed.

CHAPTER 16

I picked her up at 8 o'clock and felt great in my shiny blue car. Of course, I went inside and said hello to Jean-Claude, who was stacking dishes in the dishwasher.

"It's such a lovely evening. I thought we would take a drive in the country," I said, even though it had been Louise's idea.

Jean-Claude looked up. "Have a good time," he said, smiling.

I smelled the barbecue on my way out, remembered my miserable salad, and resented the fact that I'd had to eat alone.

"Oh, your car looks wonderful. So shiny," Louise said, and I glowed with pride.

We drove out to the countryside, through the village of *Biot* and the stone streets of Gourdon, past a stand of pines and way out across the hills. It was a beautifully clear evening, and we chatted and laughed about silly things along the way. I felt quite at ease with her by my side and wondered why I had been nervous in her company before.

"Are you comfortable?" I asked, and she smiled. "There's a rug in the back if you're cold."

I couldn't believe I finally had her in the car all to myself and we were getting along famously. I never thought that would happen again.

You're a very good driver," she said. "I feel quite safe when you're driving."

"We aim to please," I said, smiling and squeezing her hand. I was secretly thrilled that she had flattered me.

"Tell me about your work," I said, daring to get straight to the point. I glanced at her suddenly. "You are so beautiful, you must be a model."

She threw back her head and laughed. "Oh, no. I was never a model, but I did think about it at one time. I'm better off on my own now."

"So, what do you do now?

She gave a little laugh. "I'll tell you some other time."

I frowned. There it was again. She had totally evaded the question. Now I didn't know if she worked or not. What did she mean, she was better off on her own? I thought about it and decided it didn't matter in the scheme of things. But it was frustrating. Was I ever going to get the truth out of her, or was she always going to keep me at arm's length?

Dusk turned into night, the stars glinted above, and I thought we had better turn back. I was planning on asking her to join me in my apartment to see if she would come. She had never been to my apartment before, and I had imagined she was a little afraid of me. But now, after knowing her better, I realized Louise wasn't afraid of anything.

"Would you like to come in for a coffee?" I asked when we got back to Cannes. I was hoping she would say, "Yes," and had my fingers crossed in my lap.

"Yes, that would be nice," she said, and you could have knocked me over with a feather.

It seemed I didn't know her at all. I feared it would always be like this if I kept seeing her. I would think I was getting to know her, then she would spring yet another surprise on me. But she had said yes, so I was definitely going to make the most of it. It was getting late now, gone 11 o'clock, and I wondered if she might stay the night.

When we reached my apartment, I put my arm across her shoulders and turned the key in the lock. She was so tall this wasn't the most comfortable thing I have ever done, but I was determined to advance this slowly-forming relationship if I could.

My apartment was rather stuffy, so I opened a window and stared out at the starry night. It was beautiful, and the moon was a sickle-shape in the sky. I smiled to myself and thought about how I would be blessed to have a woman I was crazy about in my arms.

I made some black coffee, put my arm around her and was immediately struck by her perfume. It wasn't a flowery perfume —— I can't stand that —— it was more like a very faint musk which I adored. Louise was one of those women who never seemed to take the time to touch up her perfume or lipstick, but she always looked immaculate and smelled gorgeous. She kicked off her shoes and laid back in my arms. I could feel the weight of her body on mine and thought about what move I would make next.

We chatted for a while, and I played with her hair. She had very nice hair, not blonde exactly, but not dark either. I would say it was the shade of honey. I twisted the long curls around my finger, then gently turned her face towards mine. We kissed, and it was wonderful. Her lips were as soft as a down pillow and her tongue tasted heavenly in my mouth.

We kissed like that for a very long time, me all the while easing her closer and closer and running my fingers alongside her breast. She had marvelous breasts. I had pictured them several times in the nights when I was alone. I could imagine they were creamy white with small pink nipples. I am more of a leg man myself, but I imagined her breasts would change my mind. Soon enough, my fingers were entering the open neck of her dress and rubbing up against her bra. I put my whole hand inside and encircled one breast. It was warm and felt heavy in my hand.

My breath came quickly and the pressure of her body on my chest was almost too much to bear. I felt down her back and unzipped her dress, then unfastened her bra. She let her dress slip down her arms. Now I could clearly make out her creamy white breasts in the moonlight. I had been right; they were pale with tiny pink nipples that stood erect. I leaned over to kiss her breasts and slowly drew my tongue up the center of her body and around her nipples. Her skin tasted a little salty, which excited me even more.

Suddenly, she jumped up, pulled up her dress, and said, "Oh, my word, look at the time. I hadn't realized it was so late. Would you mind running me over to Jean-Claude's house, please?"

I sat up with a jolt. "What, you want to leave now?" I said.

She gave me an imploring look. "It's midnight, and I promised Jean-Claude I wouldn't be very late. He'll be worried about me." Then, as an afterthought, she said, "Next time we'll plan it better."

I sank back in the chair. At least, there would be a next time. Otherwise, I would be really mad at her. I am a passionate lover and have never been rejected like that before in my life. But instead of putting me off, it made me want her more and more.

CHAPTER 17

I was enjoying my time spent with Richard, and glad I had come down from Paris. We had nearly made love and I thought he would be mad at me for leaving so suddenly, but I believe in keeping a man waiting before being intimate with him. We would meet again, no doubt, then we would see where it was going. But something was bothering me and I wanted to ask my cousin about it.

Jean-Claude, was a great cook, and on Thursday night, before I went to see my father, he made a lobster dinner that was superb. He drowned the pink lobster tail in warm butter in its shell, and I mopped some of it up with a wedge of garlic baguette. We had a crisp, dry, white wine with the meal, then sat on the balcony looking out to sea with a cup of coffee. The sea was beautiful, especially in the evening when all the tourists had gone into town. The waves rolled onto shore, white and frothy, and the surface of the water gleamed in the moonlight. But I couldn't take too much sea air. It made my nose twitch. I'm not a beach person at all.

I waited for the right opportunity, then I said, "I'm worried. I'm sure Richard is cheating on me."

Jean-Claude turned to me and gave me such a funny look, I was afraid of what he might say.

"Cheating on you? Now come on, Louise. Richard is crazy about you."

I twisted my fingers in my lap, and I felt like crying. "It's the way he looks at me sometimes," I said in a small voice. "I think he's keeping a secret from me."

Jean-Claude threw his head back and laughed. "That's ridiculous. Can you hear yourself? Richard would never do a thing like that."

I tried to accept what my cousin told me, but deep down, I still didn't believe him. I knew Richard was always thinking of some other woman. It was obvious to me.

Jean-Claude furrowed his brow and gently touched my arm. "I hope you won't start these fantasies again, Louise. You know what a lot of trouble that got you into last time. I think you should see your doctor."

"I don't need to go to the doctor, Jean-Claude. I know it's true."

CHAPTER 18

I called Louise on Friday, but my call went through to voicemail. I thumped my fist on the arm of the chair. Here we go again. I thought she must be playing some annoying little game with me. I sent her a text, but she never replied. By this time, I was wondering what on earth I saw in her. She was the most infuriating woman I had ever met. First, she was available, then she wasn't, then she was again. She was very offish towards me in Paris, yet quite amenable when she came back down to Cannes. I was sure she had enjoyed our time together the other night. Now I couldn't get hold of her again.

Then, at noon, my phone pinged. It was a text from Louise. "Sorry, had to dash off. Gone back to Paris." I read it again. If it was true, she really had left and gone back home. I clenched my fists and swore. Didn't she think she owed me an explanation? Apparently not. So, according to her, we had no kind of relationship at all. She owed me nothing, and I should forget she existed.

I spent the next couple of days feeling like a fool. Somehow, I had let her use me again, and she had no qualms about it. I decided there and then I wouldn't bother with her anymore. I wouldn't try to contact her or even ask Jean-Claude how she was.

I went for a walk down *la Croisette* in the late afternoon, passing all the little cafes with their gaily colored umbrellas. I walked passed all the restaurants that I knew so well. The smells of garlic and coffee wafted on the warm breeze, and I wondered where my friends were and what they were doing. Suddenly, I felt very lonely. People, arm in arm, passed me by on the street. Groups of people sat outside the cafes, laughing together. I was heartsick.

Tourists were everywhere, ambling down the street and holding up the traffic, splashing in the sea, and playing ball on the beach, their shouts rising high above the sound of the waves. I never liked Cannes in the summer because it was so crowded. I much preferred a chilly afternoon and empty streets. But if you live in a seaside town, you expect tourists, so there was nothing I could do about that.

There was no doubt about it. I felt lost. Without Louise, I felt as if I couldn't go on and knew that was totally ridiculous. Somehow, my life had changed since meeting her. I felt lonely in my apartment and didn't know what to do to pass the time. I contemplated how she treated me once again and thought it was really too much to put up with. Would I see her again? Probably not.

When I got home, I ordered a pizza. It would save me cooking. Then, when I looked at my phone, I saw I had a text from Louise. Despite my resolution, I eagerly clicked on it.

"I'm sorry I had to dash off like that, Richard. I would have stayed longer, but something came up and I had to leave. I wonder if you might like to come up to Paris to see me. Let me know when you're coming, and I promise to be home this time."

Well, what could I possibly make of that? Apparently, I was not cast off and forgotten, after all. She wanted to see me. I have never believed in long-distance relationships before. I thought they could never work, but here I was thinking seriously about going back to Paris on the weekend. Was I mad? What made me think she would be nice to me when I got there? I might go to all that trouble, take that long drive, and have to stay in a hotel again.

My pepperoni pizza came dripping with mozzarella. I read the text again. She had asked me to come up to Paris and had promised not to be out this time. It wouldn't hurt me to take another trip. Perhaps I could get her to take me to the *Louvre* because I had never been there before.

Louise was an enigma. I found her both infuriating yet desirable. Other women seemed very dull next to her. There was no doubt about it. Louise infuriated me but I had to see her again.

CHAPTER 19

The next day I went into town to buy her a bracelet. It was a spur-of-the-moment decision, but one I thought she would appreciate. I am not great at buying jewelry for women. In fact, I had never bought jewelry for a woman before, but thought the shop assistant would help me choose something Louise would like.

I had been thinking so negatively about Louise lately. Perhaps she didn't deserve that. She wanted to see me, and that was a big plus. I would buy her something nice to show how much I cared about her.

I drove to a little jewelry store I knew on the outskirts of town and parked outside. The street was practically empty. I strode into the store and asked to see the diamond bracelets. A man with a shiny, bald head reached into a glass cabinet and presented me with an entire tray of bracelets.

I have no idea about such things, but wanted her to have the best. I saw the rows and rows of diamonds all flashing and knew I wouldn't be able to choose.

"Which one do you think my girlfriend would like?" I said, feeling my face flush.

The man unfastened one bracelet from the tray and placed it in my hand. It was beautiful. The interior was a shining gold circle, and the diamonds all around the circle winked at me under the florescent lights. I couldn't imagine that Louise wouldn't like it. Yet, I had that niggling doubt that I might choose the wrong thing or shouldn't be buying her a bracelet at all.

"Will I be able to return it if she doesn't like it?" I said because it was very expensive. He assured me that if I kept the receipt, I could bring it back.

CHAPTER 20

Paris, France

The next day, I left town with the diamond bracelet in its black velvet bag. I put it in a pocket in my carry-on bag for safekeeping.

The drive up to Paris was wonderful. Wildflowers of all different colors edged the autoroute. Red, then yellow, then fields of white flowers stretched for miles. It surprised me that there were still some wildflowers left this late in the season. I hummed a little tune and imagined what my trip to Paris might bring. Louise was a mystery, that was certain. I had never in all my life met such an unreliable woman. Jean-Claude was right. She would turn hot and cold in a flash, and she would leave you uncertain as to her motives. But never mind all that. I was going to see Louise again, and that was all that mattered. She would be delighted with my present and all would be well.

I imagined I would get further with her this time and wondered what it would be like to finally have sex. Or, I thought, smiling to myself, I would ravish her right there on her rug. I thought about the last time we had almost made love and my breath came quickly. So fast in fact, that I almost swerved because I took my eyes off the road. Louise had a ridiculous effect on me.

When I arrived in Paris, it quite surprised me to find her not only at home but amenable towards me.

"Ah, Richard, come in, come in," she said when I arrived at her door. "Did you enjoy the ride up from Cannes?"

I kissed her on both cheeks, and she smiled.

"I had a wonderful trip. The wildflowers are beautiful, even so late in the year."

"Yes, they're wonderful," she said.

I didn't really see her as a lover of nature, but when I looked around her living room, I saw several vases filled with flowers. Their scent filled the air.

I was aware of the bracelet in my carry-on and was excited to give it to her. However, I almost froze with fright, uncertain if she would like it or I would have to take it back. My heart beat fast at the thought.

"I have a present for you," I said, opening my carry-on. I pulled out the little black bag, released the drawstring, and revealed the bracelet. Then I carefully slipped it over her wrist.

I waited, my heart banging and a flush rushing to my cheeks. Would she like it? I was so afraid she wouldn't.

She swished it this way and that way, watching the diamonds flash in the sunny room, and finally said, "I love it, darling. It's beautiful."

I could breathe again. I had chosen well, and she loved it. I couldn't be happier.

That night, she let me share her bed. I climbed in between the silky white sheets and cuddled her close to my body. I could feel the warmth of her breath on my chest. She was wearing a long, white nightdress made of lace and I thought I would try to ease it up her legs. But when I grasped the lacy cloth, she said, "I'm tired, Richard, let's sleep."

I lay there and stared at the ceiling in the darkness. I had hoped she would be more willing since I had brought her a present. But never mind, I would wait. It would be worth it, I felt sure.

CHAPTER 21

The next day we went to the *Louvre* and, apart from all the wretched tourists, it was a very interesting trip. I had never seen the Mona Lisa and was immediately struck by her extraordinary smile. She reminded me of Louise. How a woman could completely disarm a man with her smile and leave him squirming and out of breath was unfathomable to me.

It turned out that Louise was a wonderful cook —— she had a talent for making a meal special. She lit a pair of red candles in crystal candle holders and arranged a small posy of flowers in the center of the table. A heavenly smell filled the air when she brought over a dish of chicken breasts covered in a creamy cheese sauce over noodles. It was a plain enough meal, but the way Louise prepared it with small sprigs of parsley on the top was magnificent. Then there was a chocolate *ganache* to follow. The two bottles of Burgundy that we consumed had an amazing effect on me. I felt so mellow and could only dream of the night ahead.

When Louise was sitting on the couch, I put my arm around her shoulders. She snuggled up, and I felt hot all over. I kissed the top of her head and whispered in her ear. "I think I am falling in love with you, Louise." She kissed me in answer. I had hoped she would say something like that to me, but she didn't. We stayed up talking until 1 o'clock, by which time I was slightly tired. But I was determined not to sleep because I badly wanted to make love to her.

After a nice, mellow glass of brandy, we went into the bedroom, and she put on her lace nightdress while I undressed and slipped into bed. I watched intently while she removed her false eyelashes, arranged them in a little box, and wiped her face with a cotton ball. She then ran a brush through her hair. I am a patient man, but by this time, I was totally beside myself with desire.

When Louise finally came to bed, I held her in my arms, and we kissed for a long time. I felt her probing tongue in my mouth, and it made my crotch tingle. If we didn't make love this time, I would simply lose my mind. I kissed her eyelids and the lobes of her ears, and vowed I would make her squirm with desire because I wanted to please her and show her how much I loved her.

Her hair was loose and spread across my chest. I ran my fingers through the strands and kissed the top of her head. All the while she was making snuffling noises like a little animal, snuggling closer and closer to me, her face hot on my neck. My breath came quickly as I felt her breasts pressing softly against me. They were warm beneath the lacy cloth of her nightdress. When I pulled her nightdress up over her knees, she lifted herself off the pillow for me to pull it over her head.

Now I had her warm, naked body next to mine. It felt like heaven, and I could tell she was almost ready for me to penetrate her. I played with her breasts, tugging softly at her nipples with my teeth and making them stand erect. She reached down and pushed her hand between my legs, and I moaned with joy. I gasped when she gently slid one leg over my hips and rubbed up against my body. "What do you like best?" I asked her softly, and in answer, she took my trembling hand and placed it gently inside the top of her thigh. The feel of her moist skin beneath my fingers was intoxicating.

Afterwards, we cuddled and kissed, and I rolled back on my side and looked at her properly. Her hair was all in disarray, but she looked wonderful. Her brown eyes were mesmerizing, and her lips parted when I touched her cheek. I had never seen such a beautiful woman in all my life. I felt sure she was the woman I was meant to be with for all eternity. I realized I was madly in love with her, and it was almost painful. Then I totally surprised myself by climbing out of bed, going down on one knee, and asking her to marry me.

"Yes," she said, and we both laughed.

I got back into bed and lay next to her. My heart was thumping so hard in my chest I could almost hear it. Then, when I tried to sleep, I suddenly realized I must have been out of my mind. I had vowed never to risk marriage again after Colette, and Louise was the most infuriating woman I had ever met. But I really wanted to be with her. I couldn't bear the thought of her with anybody else.

CHAPTER 22

We arranged to be married in a registry office in Paris. Louise didn't want to wear white, so she bought a tight-fitting, coral-colored dress with matching shoes and an outlandish white hat. Since I hadn't thought I would stay so long in Paris, I didn't bring many clothes with me. Now I had to go into town and buy something smart to wear for my wedding. I bought a dark suit with a blue satin shirt, and when Louise told me I was a handsome groom, I felt my face flush with pride. I loved to be complimented by my darling Louise.

"Are you going to ask your father to attend the wedding?" I asked.

She looked up from her copy of Vogue and said, "Jean-Claude will give me away."

I couldn't understand it at all. There must have been some rift in the family. I didn't ask about her mother, as it seemed she wouldn't be coming either. I had nobody on my side of the family, either. My sister, Amy, would have come up from Kent, but she wasn't well, so I didn't like to ask her.

We married two weeks later, and Louise ordered massive

bunches of fragrant white roses to be arranged in the registry office. I thought it was very extravagant, and told her so, but she insisted she wanted them, and it was her money, after all.

Jean-Claude flew up to Paris for the day and looked splendid in his dark gray suit and blue tie.

"I'm so glad you could come and give me away," Louise told him, and I thought it was very odd indeed.

"For richer or for poorer. In sickness and in health, ——" the Registrar droned on. I was so excited, I hardly heard him say the words. I didn't know at the time how those words would come back to haunt me. We swapped rings, then we were husband and wife.

Two friends of Louise's came to witness the wedding, and as we didn't have a photographer, one of them took pictures of us on the steps of the registry office. A little crowd had gathered outside and cheered when we came out. A small girl came up and put her hand on Louise's dress. Her mother rushed up, pulled the child away, and apologized profusely.

When we got back to the apartment, I carried my new bride over the threshold and we both fell laughing onto the bed. She gave me the task of undoing the tiny, fiddly buttons that ran down the entire back of her dress. It was quite a job, and I had to give up halfway, so she slid out of the dress and hung it on a hanger. I wanted her there and then, but knew she would be mad if I spoiled her hair. Louise liked to do things her way, so I waited for her to sit down at the dressing table, take off her make-up and brush her hair, then we went to bed. I drowned her in kisses all over her body. I kissed her lips, her breasts, and down between her legs. She lifted her hips and moaned with pleasure. It was the happiest day of my life.

But then came the practicalities. Where should we live? Which apartment was more convenient? I had no interest in living in Paris. I couldn't stand the traffic, and the noise was too much for me —— taxi cabs honking at all hours of the day and night and drunks singing in the streets.

But Louise didn't want to live in Cannes. "It's too near the sea," she said.

"I love the sea," I said. "I would miss it if we lived in Paris."

I had to admit my apartment was rather small for a married couple, but I loved Cannes and could see Louise fitting in quite well. Mentally, I noted I would have to get rid of some of my stuff because I was a bit of a hoarder, and the apartment was full of old things. I didn't know what to do about that because I liked to keep things I might use one day. My newspapers and magazines dated back years. Somehow, I would have to part with them if I wanted to make room for Louise.

"You'll be able to see more of Jean-Claude," I said, thinking that would lure her to Cannes.

For a minute, I thought she was going to cry, but instead, she said, “Alright, we’ll live in Cannes, but if it doesn’t work out, we’ll move back to Paris.”

I was delighted. My Louise. My life was about to change for the better. Or so I thought.

CHAPTER 23

Cannes, France

Louise had many possessions to sell, so it took some time to get her to move to Cannes.

"You have a lot of artwork," I said, and dreaded trying to find a place on the walls for all her paintings. I liked her dramatic paintings of the sea, and some of the portraits, but couldn't understand the squares and circles of the abstract art at all. But she liked them, so I made room for them on the walls. She also brought masses of linen and tablecloths.

"When are we going to use all this linen, Louise?"

"Well, you have so many books," she said, grinning. "I've never seen so many books in one place before, except in a library."

She looked around the room and made a face. "This apartment is way too small for us. What will we do when we have a family?"

"We shall have to think about that later," I said.

Louise became the perfect wife and went out of her way to please me. She was so diligent, in fact, that I wondered how I had ever lived without her. She quickly got into a routine of mixing my two glasses of whiskey soda in the evening and served me breakfast on a tray in bed. Her eggs Benedict were perfect; nicer than ones you would get in the best hotels. And her bagels with cream cheese and sliced, smoked salmon were to die for.

She knew I loved to smoke occasionally, so she bought me a humidor made of red leather filled with good quality cigars. I lit them in the evenings and lay back, watching the smoke curl in the air.

Louise always liked to surprise me, and I usually like to be surprised, but sometimes her surprises were not to my liking. One day we were having dinner on the balcony of my apartment —— I should say our apartment, but that took a while to get used to —— and she said something I hadn't expected.

"I'm going to be out all day tomorrow, darling. I shall leave you something cold in the fridge."

I listened with surprise. She had never been away on her own before, never expressed a desire. It wasn't that she should stay at home, of course. I was just not used to her going away.

"Where are you going?"

"A friend of mine in Paris needs help with some shopping. She is going to an important dance and wants me to help her choose a dress."

I didn't quite know what to make of that. Did her friend really need someone to go all that way to help her choose a dress? It seemed very odd to me, but Louise wanted it, so she must have her day out.

"That's fine," I said, quite relieved to hear it was something innocent, like shopping with a friend. I didn't ask her which friend she was referring to because I didn't know any of them well. "What time will you be home?"

She was silent for a moment, then said, "It's best that I call you when I'm through."

"You don't want me to pick you up at the airport?"

"No, I can easily catch a cab."

So, Louise went away on Friday morning, and I had the cold supper she left in the fridge. Sliced ham with a green salad was to my liking, but the salad was tasteless, eating alone. I picked at the lettuce and the tomatoes, popped a couple of olives in my mouth, and ate the ham slices. Then I was done. The white wine I chose didn't seem to go with the meal, but I suspected it was because Louise wasn't sharing a glass or two with me.

The apartment felt empty without her. My footsteps

echoed every time I moved around. Louise breathed life into a space. She wore her long, green robe in the house and often sang in her lovely soprano voice as she went about her chores. She fluttered from room to room like a beautiful butterfly and had a presence that was lovely. The time passed slowly, and I couldn't settle down. It was the first time I had been alone since our marriage, and it seemed only right that she should be there with me now.

After dinner, I got into my pajamas and lay on the couch. I clicked through the TV channels, but there was nothing worth watching, so I went to bed. It was getting late, but there was no sign of Louise. I got out of bed and peered out of the window, hoping I would see the taxi pull up outside. It was very dark now, except for the streetlamps and the twinkling stars, and there wasn't a soul about. The street had an eerie look to it that night. The pools of light from the street lamps shone down on the empty sidewalks and gave them a ghostly, yellow glow. I had never looked at the street properly at night before, and the emptiness of it made me nervous. I could have been the only person left on the planet.

I crept back into bed and turned out the light. It was strange that she was out so late, and I hadn't heard from her. I immediately turned on the light, grabbed my phone, and texted her. "When are you coming home? I miss you."

She soon replied, "I'm on my way, darling." But I didn't

know if she was still on the plane, at the airport, or driving home in a cab. Without Louise, I felt adrift, like a boat lost at sea. I needed Louise beside me. I loved her so much.

I went back to bed and fell asleep. Louise came in at about 11 o'clock and, after a cup of coffee, joined me in bed.

"How did your day go?" I asked sleepily. "Did your friend find a suitable dress?"

She snuggled up against me, and I put my arm around her and kissed her lips.

"She really had no idea what she wanted, so I chose one for her. It's a pale lemon color, long, with puff sleeves. She looked charming."

"I was going to wait up for you," I said, "but it's been a long day, and I was tired."

Now that Louise was home and safe, I fell asleep and completely forgot about her trip.

We had Jean-Claude round for dinner the next night and Louise cooked a dish of chicken breast sliced thinly, dipped in flour and fried.

Jean-Claude loved the meal. "I really miss your cooking, Louise."

I felt sorry for him living alone and told him quite often that he needed a wife. But he was forty-four now and I couldn't see him ever settling down. But then, of course, I hadn't thought of settling down, either, but here I was with the most beautiful woman I had ever seen. I took Louise's hand under the table and smiled at her. "You are the best cook in the world, my wonderful wife."

We made love as soon as Jean-Claude was gone.

CHAPTER 24

Sometime later, I started noting my wife's spending habits. I nearly died when she kept bringing in more and more artwork —— scenes of Paris by night and portraits of curvy women. She certainly had good taste, but there was no place on the walls, and I was perfectly happy with the artwork we already had.

"Why are you buying all these paintings, Louise?"

She looked up from her book. "I thought you liked them."

"It's not a matter of liking them. We have no room for them."

"I hope you aren't going to be petty all the time, questioning me about every little thing," she said and pouted her lips.

Then there were the dresses, the hats, and the skimpy, black underwear, but mainly it was the shoes. She bought so many pairs of shoes.

"Haven't you got enough shoes, Louise?" I snapped one day.

"I enjoy buying shoes. They make me happy."

"I can't see why you need a pair for every outfit. Why not buy some white shoes and wear them with the dresses you have in your closet?"

Then one day, she came home with a pair of dark green, alligator -skin shoes.

"Tell me how much you paid for those shoes," I said, rather sharply.

She scoffed at me and ignored what I said.

Then when the mail came, I steamed open a letter from her bank and carefully looked at her statement. I gasped. The money she spent on shoe shopping was ridiculous. I put the statement back, ran my thumb across the steamed envelope, and laid it on the dresser where I had found it.

CHAPTER 25

One day, when I was alone in the apartment, I looked at Richard's computer, but I couldn't get it to open as I didn't have the password. I tried everything. I punched in his birthday, our address, my birthday, nothing worked. The computer just wouldn't open.

I was certain he was keeping something from me. He had a secret, that was for sure. I had thought he was having an affair before we married, now I was certain of it. He gave me a very impersonal look sometimes as if he was thinking of her. I knew he couldn't wait to see her again. He was probably in bed with her right now.

I paced up and down the living room, wondering what I should do next. I picked up a heavy glass paperweight and rolled it round in my hand. What would happen if I flung it at his head? Would he die? Would I be sorry? I had a picture in my mind of Richard lying on the floor, the aqua-blue paperweight beside him, and his head split open. He was lying in a pool of blood. Could I really do that to him? Was I mad?

Just then, the front door clicked open, and Richard came in. He put his arm around me and kissed my lips, but I pulled away. He had bought some bread and placed the baguette on the counter. The smell of the freshly baked bread was wonderful, but I looked at the loaf, then at him, and thought it was a good ploy. He would be smart enough to think of getting bread, so I wouldn't be suspicious. But I was.

"You've been to see your lover, haven't you?" I said with a vengeance.

"Don't be ridiculous, Louise. I went out to get some bread."

"That's what you tell me. But I know you have another woman, Richard. You've been gone for a very long time."

"What are you talking about? I love you."

I wanted to believe him, but could see he was lying. His hands shook ever so slightly, and his lip quivered. Surely, that was proof enough.

CHAPTER 26

The next day when Louise was out, I sat in the window seat in the sun and called Jean-Claude. At first, the phone just rang and rang, but then he answered.

"Hi, Richard, how's things?"

I glanced out of the window into the garden and saw two little sparrows in the bird bath kicking up water for all they were worth. "I have a problem, Jean-Claude. It's about Louise."

There was silence, then he asked me what I meant. I felt a little foolish now when I thought of Louise's accusation. It was quite ridiculous.

"Louise thinks I'm having an affair," I said.

I thought he might laugh, but he didn't. In fact, he was quite serious when he said, "I was afraid this would happen."

"What do you mean?"

There was a silence, then he said slowly, "Louise is a sick woman. I should have warned you before you got married."

I looked out at the birdbath, but the little birds had flown away.

“A sick woman?”

“Yes, mental illness runs in her family. Her mother had to go into a mental hospital for a year once and it was a terrible blow to Louise. She was only eleven at the time.”

“What was wrong with her mother?”

Jean-Claude went quiet for a minute, and I wondered what he was going to say. “They never said what the problem was, but she tried to kill Louise’s father with a bread knife.”

I gasped. What a horrible story. So, this was why Louise never mentioned her mother. There was a family secret she was hiding from me. I wondered if she really had inherited her mother’s illness. If her mother was still alive, where did she live? What was our future likely to be? I had so many questions; I didn’t know what I would do.

My first instinct was to blame Jean-Claude. Why hadn’t he told me this before? He should have told me about the family secret himself. But then, would I have told someone who was about to marry? He must have known I wouldn’t listen to him.

“What should I do about it?” I asked.

“There’s not much you can do about it, but wait for her bouts of paranoia to pass. She won't go to a doctor. I know. I've tried that before."

"This is a very bad omen," I said and had a terrible feeling this was only half of the story.

CHAPTER 27

A few weeks later, Louise gave me another surprise.

"I have to go to Paris on Friday," she said. "My friend's mother died quite suddenly, and I've got to go to the funeral."

"Which friend is that?" I asked.

"Oh, you wouldn't know her, but we have been friends for years. I met her long before we married."

"Why don't I come with you?" I said, to see what she would say.

"That's very sweet of you, darling, but I won't put you to all that trouble. You know how you hate flying and you don't enjoy going to Paris at all."

So, the next day, Louise went out shopping for the funeral. She bought a little black dress that came down to just below her knees and accentuated her figure. The shoes to match had little bows on the front. I complemented her on her good taste.

Then, when I was alone, I thought I would have a quick look in Louise's closet. She'd been shopping all the time lately, and

I wanted to know what she bought. I crept stealthily into the bedroom as if she was in the apartment and might be watching me.

When I looked in the closet, I saw rows of clothes neatly arranged on hangers and color coded. Some of her clothes still had their price tags on them. Then I looked up and saw all the boxes of shoes, piled high to the roof of the closet, I thought Louise must have to stand on a chair to get them down. I shuddered to think how many shoes were in those boxes and what they must have cost. I shut the door quickly and walked away. Then it occurred to me that I hadn't looked at the floor of the closet where there were yet more boxes. Perhaps she had even more shoes.

I could have sworn she was watching me when I went back into the bedroom, but I was determined to find out what was in that closet. I flung open the door, saw the clothes all lined up and the umpteen boxes of shoes at the top, and there, at the bottom in the corner, were other boxes I had noticed but not looked at. When I opened them up, my eyes nearly popped out of my head. Those boxes were full of baby clothes.

I picked up a little white dress. It was cotton with a frilly neckline, and a satin-edged hem, and felt very small in my hands. There were also little, one-piece outfits that had snaps at the bottom, and many bibs in all different colors with kittens and puppies embroidered on them. She had also bought little crocheted hats and mittens to suit a baby.

I didn't know Louise was collecting baby clothes. I thought about our lovemaking and remembered that Louise was thirty-eight, so wanting a baby was only natural, but we hadn't discussed it at all. Surely, babies were a decision two people should make, and here was Louise collecting baby clothes, hoping she would become pregnant.

I realized perhaps I should think about having a family now before it was too late. At forty-two, I was getting old to be a father and if we were going to have children, we better start trying soon. The funny thing was, I had gone all those years without giving children a second thought.

Then I thought more deeply about the situation. Should we really plan to have children at all if Louise was ill? It could be a big problem. She might have difficulties bringing up a baby, and the baby could also inherit her disease. I really wanted her to go to the doctor, but couldn't see that happening.

I wasn't sure how to progress with this. If I had it out with her, she would know I had been snooping in her closet. Should I tell her how scared I was she wouldn't be able to cope with a baby? That might make her angry. Should I risk her anger rather than bring a child into the world? I didn't know what to do.

CHAPTER 28

A month later, we were lying together on the balcony in the sun when Louise said, "I have to go to Paris on Friday, darling. My friend is getting married."

I was shocked. Who was this friend? Was it the friend whose mother had died, and who had to have a dress for the dance? Or was it someone else entirely? The fact was, I didn't know her friends. There was the couple at the wedding, of course. They seemed very nice, but we hadn't spoken much at all.

"I really should go with you this time. Your friend will think it odd if you turn up on your own."

But Louise was adamant. "No, darling. Why would you want to go to a stranger's wedding? And you know you hate flying. You would be perfectly miserable."

She was right again. I didn't know her friend. It seemed ridiculous now that I thought about it. I dropped the subject and never mentioned it when Louise went shopping for more clothes. This time she bought a dress in the palest pink, almost white, with matching shoes and a little pink hat. She looked beautiful.

“How was the wedding?” I asked her when she got back.

She suddenly looked up, and her lip quivered as if I had caught her off-guard. “Oh, my friend was a beautiful bride,” she said. “I vaguely knew her husband, so it was nice to talk to him again. I think I shall go see them when they get back from their honeymoon.

All these trips to Paris and all these new clothes. The whole thing was grating on my nerves. Why did she keep this friend a secret? What had she got to hide? Yet, to be honest, I hated Paris and was glad I never had to go there again.

The funny thing was she continued to take trips up to Paris every month, and I suddenly realized it was always on Fridays. It happened again and again with all kinds of excuses; she was going to a spa with a friend; she wanted to go to the art gallery, and once she had to go to another funeral.

What could I say? She was a grown woman. She could come and go as she pleased, but I wondered when she would go away next and what excuse she would have for me then. I thought it was very odd, and it made me uncomfortable. Why couldn’t she spend her time with me instead of trooping off to Paris to see all these old friends I’d never met?

Then it occurred to me she had a lover. I was horrified. Why hadn’t I thought of that before? Surely, she was slipping out on Fridays and meeting some other man somewhere. He may have been an old boyfriend in Paris, for all I knew. I imagined Louise with a lover and thumped my fist on the table. Surely, this wasn't going on under my nose and I had been taken in by it all this time. But why did she go on Fridays every month? It made no sense. If she had a lover, surely, she would want to see him more often than once a month. She would think up more plausible reasons to leave town.

I called Jean-Claude and asked him outright about Louise and her Friday visits. I knew she confided in her cousin, so he would be able to solve the mystery.

"Do you know why Louise goes away on Fridays every month?" I asked. "Has she told you anything about her outings?"

"No, she doesn't talk to me about such things," he said, and I didn't believe him at all. "She is probably going shopping."

I took a deep breath. "You don't think she has a lover, do you?"

Jean-Claude laughed. "Oh, no, I would know about it if she had a lover. She would have told me. Louise is very faithful; I am sure of it. Don't worry about such things."

That was enough for me. I had to believe him, so I put it out of my mind.

CHAPTER 29

One day we were having a crusty baguette and brie for lunch in the kitchen when Louise said out of the blue, "I want to have a baby."

Of course, I knew this was coming, but I had conveniently put it out of my mind. I took my time in answering her. My mind was filled with the idea that Louise wouldn't be able to cope with a baby and it would be a disaster. I saw her getting irritable with the baby, not taking care of it, and I wondered what I should say.

"Now may not be the right time. We've only been married a few months and, after all, we're just getting to know each other."

"It's not too soon. I've always wanted a baby, and I'm thirty-eight years old."

"I think we should leave it a bit longer," I said. "Just until we are more settled."

She sounded like a petulant child, and pouted when she said, "But I want to start trying now. Who knows how long it might take?"

I was running out of excuses and could feel my face flush. "What if I said I didn't want a baby at all. What would you say about that?"

She gave me a piercing look. "I want a baby now, Richard. I'm going to come off the pill and see what happens."

So that was decided. Before long, we could be the parents of a little, innocent baby and who knew what would happen then? But I loved Louise to distraction and wanted to make her happy. I would keep a keen eye on her health to see if she had any more bouts of paranoia. I didn't quite know what I would do if she got sick again, but I would help her in any way I could.

CHAPTER 30

Dijon, France

Then the very next month, Louise told me she was going away again. She gave me some flimsy excuse this time, and I didn't believe her. I was furious and jealous at the same time. What if Jean-Claude had been wrong, and she really did have a lover?

She told me she was driving up to Paris because they had canceled her flight due to bad weather. So, when she was about to leave, I was ready. This time, I didn't ask her to justify her trip. I followed her. I was scared about what I would find, but I badly wanted to know why she went to Paris every month.

The weather was terrible, not conducive to a long drive from Cannes to Paris. The rain came down in sheets in front of the windshield and, at one point, I could barely see the road in front of me. I squinted through the windshield wipers and skirted round the lines of trucks, keeping my distance from Louise. Cars overtook me in my lane, water flying off their wheels. I was exhausted and wanted to stop and rest, but of course, I had to push on if I was to see where she was going.

Then after many kilometers, Louise took a fork in the road to the northeast on the *autoroute*. I couldn't believe it. I thought, perhaps, she knew a better way to get to Paris by avoiding all the traffic. I pressed on behind her and watched the kilometers fall away. Then I had the sudden realization we weren't going toward Paris at all. We were heading for Dijon. I was dumbstruck when I saw the sign on the side of the road. What was she going to do in Dijon? Had she been going there all along? Then I remembered back to when we first met, and she told me she was in Dijon. I remembered how surprised I was then. Did she have a lover there?

After some time on the *autoroute*, we got to Dijon. I kept back but left enough room between our cars so that I could see where she went. She took twists and turns all around the city and finally parked the car in a nearly empty, tree-lined street. I stopped abruptly some distance away and waited to see what she would do next.

She got out of the car, put up her umbrella, and ran up to a huge gray building on the corner. When she disappeared under the big archway, I got out of the car and went to see where she'd gone. I looked up at the sign over the archway and gasped. It said Dijon prison. What on earth was my dear Louise doing visiting someone in prison?

I waited and waited, but she was gone for quite a while. In the end, I decided to leave before she came out and drove back to Cannes. On the long drive home, I tried to understand what she was doing visiting someone in prison. This was completely strange to me. I had no idea what she was up to. I vowed to make her tell me what it was all about when we got home. More than likely, all those Friday trips to see her friends in Paris were fake. Instead, she was going to Dijon to see someone in prison. I gritted my teeth and scowled.

At least she didn't have a lover. I wouldn't know what to do about that. But visiting a prison every month! This was yet another one of Louise's surprises, and not a nice one at that.

Then I realized I couldn't very well ask her what she was doing visiting someone in prison because she would then know that I had followed her. Now I was stuck. I didn't know how I should broach the subject.

CHAPTER 31

This time when I went away, I thought it was strange that Richard didn't ask me where I was going He always wanted to interrogate me. But this time was different and I was quite worried about it. What was Richard thinking? Did he know about my trips to Dijon. I vowed I would never tell him and would deny it if he asked.

I had driven all the way from Cannes to Dijon in the pouring rain. My eyes were tired from staring through the windshield, and I was exhausted. When I got out of the car, the rain was coming down in torrents and splashing into the puddles on the pavement. I looked at my watch and realized that visiting time would soon be over, and if I didn't hurry now, I would be too late.

It was good to get out of the rain, but my feet in my new red shoes were soaking wet. I entered the building and made my way to the visitor's lounge. They knew me there as I had been visiting for years.

"*Bonjour*, Madam."

"*Bonjour*."

At first, I didn't visit my father at all because I was so angry with him for what he'd done. I couldn't understand it, and it was more than I could bear. I agonized over the decision to see him for many years and completely ignored him for some time. But they said he was not in a healthy frame of mind when he committed the crime, so I started visiting him in the prison. I knew he was being punished, but I hated him for how he had ruined my life. But he was my father, after all. I couldn't let him rot in prison without a friend on the outside.

He was crying when I walked into the little room with the glass screen. It was terrible to see him like that. I had never seen my father cry before, and I didn't know what to say. His hair was thinning on top and it was now gray, and in some spots it was white. It was long and needed cutting. I sat silently for a while, watching him sitting there behind the glass partition with his head in his hands, sobbing.

He was looking more and more gaunt each time I visited him. He was getting old and was wasting away in prison. But he had done a terrible thing, and he had to pay for his sins. Whenever I looked at him, I wanted to feel a great love, but rather than that, I just felt angry. The anger didn't seem to want to leave me. I had thought about counseling for some time because it was hard to cope with my emotions. But in the end, I didn't go because I didn't want to talk about it with a stranger.

My father was always pleased to see me, and I tried to imagine what his life was like behind bars. Did they eat proper meals? Did they get recreation outside of their cells? I had asked him about these things before, but he was evasive about what went on in the prison.

"I've been a terrible father to you, Louise. And you've been such a faithful daughter."

"That's all behind us now, Papa. Let's not talk about it again."

I had a lump in my throat. In all the years since I had been visiting him, he had never shown an ounce of remorse. He had always been quite stoic. He continued to sob behind the glass, and when he looked up, I could see streaks of tears running down his face. I had forgiven him for what he did, but not forgotten.

I knew I should put it behind me now, but it was difficult. As I twisted my fingers in my lap, I wanted to beat my fists on the glass to show him how angry I was. But I realized at the same time it would be pointless. What could either of us do about it now?

I thought of Richard and what he would say if he knew I came to the prison every month instead of going to Paris like I said. He would know I was a liar. But I couldn't tell him about my father. It was impossible. Visiting my father had to remain a secret.

CHAPTER 32

Cannes, France

That night, before Louise got home, I called my friend Jean-Claude. I had been thinking about what I would say to him and felt embarrassed by what I had done. I had fooled Louise by following her to Dijon, but she had lied to me. What was I supposed to do?

"Do you have any idea why Louise keeps going to Dijon?" I asked him.

Jean-Claude was very cagey, and I could tell he didn't want to talk about it.

"How did you know she goes to Dijon?"

"I followed her."

Now I had said it. My hands shook as I admitted to Louise's cousin that I had followed her. Jean-Claude would now know I knew where she went. I felt underhanded somehow. I felt bad for doubting her word. But she hadn't told me anything. She should have shared the information with me long ago, then I wouldn't have had to find out the hard way. Now I knew I was married to a liar.

There was silence on the end of the line, then he said, "We should get together soon to talk about this. I don't think we should discuss it on the phone. How about coming round for a glass of wine on Monday afternoon?"

We agreed to meet up on the following Monday and I was relieved because I dearly wanted to know what Louise was up to.

CHAPTER 33

It was a crisp autumn day, and all the leaves were changing color along *La Croisette*. But I was in no mood to think about the trees when I went to see Jean-Claude on Monday afternoon. His door was open, so I walked right in and found him in the living room, working on his computer.

"Hi," he said. "Let's go outside and get some fresh air."

He opened the doors to the balcony, and we sat outside looking out to sea. The waters were quite calm, and the sun made the froth on the waves sparkle like diamonds. I watched some children building sandcastles on the beach.

Jean-Claude said, "I'll get some wine."

He got up and went inside to get the wine, and while he was away, I wondered how I should broach the subject of Louise. I had an inkling that he thought I was underhanded following her to Dijon, but I really wanted to know what she was doing there and who she was visiting. He came back with the drinks on a tray, and put it on the little table beneath the multi-colored umbrella. The wine was a good claret, and I wished I could have enjoyed it under different circumstances.

"I have found out about Louise's monthly trips to Dijon," I said. "She isn't going to Paris at all. She's been lying to me all along."

Jean-Claude whistled through his teeth. "Did you see where she went?"

"Yes, she was visiting someone in the prison."

Jean-Claude was looking out to sea. "And did she tell you who it was?"

"No, and I can't ask because she would be horrified if she knew I had followed her."

I looked at him and wondered what to say next. Perhaps he disapproved of me following Louise.

"Tell me who she's visiting," I said.

Jean-Claude traced his finger round the rim of his glass and for a long while he was silent. I tapped my foot impatiently, waiting for an answer.

"It's like this," he said. "Louise has a shady past, and she doesn't want people knowing about it."

"But, I'm not people, I'm her husband," I said forcefully. I clenched my fist under the table and could feel the familiar flush coming to my face.

Jean-Claude looked into his wine glass for a long time and sighed. "She visits her father every month," he said, and stared at me to see my reaction.

"What!"

Well, this was the worst surprise that could have been sprung upon me. To say it shocked me would be an understatement. Now I wish I had talked to her more about her parents. I was finding out all kinds of things about her family. I remembered back to when we had met Mylan in the cafe down by the port. Louise had changed the subject when he'd asked her about her father.

Jean-Claude leaned back in his chair and folded his arms across his chest, "Pierre Dumas killed his wife, Louise's mother, and they gave him a life sentence."

CHAPTER 34

I drove home feeling absolutely shattered. Of all the secrets Louise had, I could never have guessed she went to see her father in prison. We shouldn't have to hide such things from each other. I would have told her anything about my past if she had asked me. I scoffed. But, of course, I didn't have a shady past, so I didn't mind talking about it. I tried to understand Louise's attitude, but still couldn't see why she hadn't shared her secret with me. It wasn't her fault that her father had done such a terrible thing. She was only a child when it happened.

I imagined my poor Louise when she was a young girl. She had to live with two people who weren't fit to be parents. She'd had a terrible childhood, which might explain her strange moods. Her mother was mentally ill, and her father was a murderer. I couldn't imagine anything worse than that.

Now I didn't know what to do. She would be furious with me if she knew I had followed her to Dijon and watched her go into the prison. But she would be even more furious if she thought I had been discussing her trips with Jean-Claude. She might see that as unforgivable. I would feel on edge the whole time around her now. With this news, I knew I wouldn't be able to relax at all.

CHAPTER 35

When I got home, I went online and Googled Pierre Dumas in *Dijon Prison.* I found the *Dijon Chronicle* and there he was. Pierre Dumas who was spending life in prison for poisoning his wife with thallium. I gasped. So that was the whole sordid story. I read the article, and it said that Louise had once tried to get him out of prison, but she had been unsuccessful. It said the governor of the prison had been informed, but Pierre Dumas would not get time off for good behavior.

Next, I looked up thallium. It surprised me to find that it was an ingredient found in rat poison. It had no smell or taste. I could see how easy it would be to kill someone with thallium. Did he really hate his wife that much? Did he despise her so much that he wanted to kill her and make her suffer in that way? She must have been a terrible wife, surely?

Now that I knew about Louise, I looked upon her differently. She was the daughter of a murderer, after all. I thought of Pierre Dumas in the prison at Dijon and wondered how he filled his days. I didn't know about prison life and found that I didn't feel sorry for him at all. Even if his wife lied to him like Louise lied to me, it wasn't reason enough to poison her.

And if his wife came at him with a knife when she was ill, I'm sure he was stronger than her and could easily take the knife away from her. It was all too much. I couldn't understand it.

But should I tell Louise about my find? Should I come clean? I agonized over this question for days. Then I decided I would keep that information to myself, so I never mentioned it to her.

The monthly trips continued, and I suffered all the explanations, knowing that she was lying to me. I hated liars, yet here I was living with the worst liar of all. Could I see her point of view? Could I see why she kept her past a secret from me? I thought about this for some time, but it baffled me.

CHAPTER 36

Then one day, I snapped. I found her in the kitchen scrubbing carrots, putting them one at a time into a pot of water. I was so mad; I trembled. She had her back to me, so I pulled her up from her chair, grasped her arm, and spun her round to face me.

"You're hurting me!" she cried out.

"You've been lying to me, Louise, and like a fool I've put up with it all this time."

"Get your hands off of me."

I let her go and realized I hadn't thought out what I was going to say next. But suddenly, all that didn't matter. I would not be lied to anymore.

"I know about your trips to Dijon," I said, and her eyes grew wide. "You've not been going to Paris at all. You've been lying to me every month, haven't you?"

My heart banged in my chest, and I clenched my fist over and over again.

"I don't know what you're talking about."

"I know all about your father."

She looked at me with eyes shining. "How do you know?"

"I followed you."

She pummeled her fists on my chest. "How dare you follow me. How dare you?"

"I know why your father is in prison." It was agony for me to say the words. I knew they would upset her, but I didn't care at that moment. I wanted her to pay for her lies. "I know all about what he did to your mother."

She suddenly plopped down on the chair and dropped her head in her hands. I thought she was going to cry, but when she looked up, her face was scarlet with rage. "You have no idea what I've been through. I had to watch my mother when she was ill. I was only a little girl, and I didn't understand what was happening. My mother was taken away from me for a year, and I lost my best friend."

I felt guilty. Even though I knew she had been lying, I could see why. What would I have done if I were in the same position as Louise? I thought I would have come clean ages ago, but you never know what you will do until you are in that same situation. "I'm sorry that happened to you," I said.

She was crying now, and I could hardly hold back the tears myself.

"I loved my mother so much, and I had to watch her die. I saw her writhing in pain on the floor. I heard her crying out. And there was nothing I could do. Then they took my father to prison. I couldn't understand why he had done such a wicked thing. I couldn't understand it at all!"

I sat down at the table beside her and put my arm around her heaving shoulders. She turned and buried her face in my chest. Her tears instantly wet my shirt, and her weeping clawed at my heart. I rocked her like a baby for a long time. The clock on the wall chimed the hour, and I forgave her for all her lies.

CHAPTER 37

Time passed, winter came, and we spent time together planning for a baby. I hoped Louise wouldn't have any more of her psychotic, paranoid thoughts, so I watched her carefully. Three months went by, and Louise didn't get pregnant. We talked about going to see a gynecologist, but I dissuaded her. I reminded her she was trying for a baby late in life, so it would take over three months to get pregnant. She was distraught. We had tears on more than one occasion, and when she got her period, she was so depressed she hardly spoke to me for days.

Once I found her on the bed crying and my heart contracted. I knew I loved my wife, and I wanted to get her pregnant for her sake. I made love to her as much as I could, but I have to say even that became a problem. Sometimes I couldn't get an erection and that was cause for more tears. Louise was determined to get pregnant, and I was the only one who could help her fulfill her dream.

Then, two months later, she missed her period. She rushed up to me with the news and took a pregnancy test. Yes, the white stripe on the wand turned blue, and she shrieked with delight.

She went to the doctor, and he confirmed she was having a baby.

When Louise was pregnant, I took it upon myself to take extra care of her. I helped her by filling the dishwasher, vacuuming the floor, and cooking the meals when she was tired. She was happy, and that was all that mattered. She was my Queen.

Then, one day at her monthly checkup, the doctor told her that her blood pressure was far too high, and it might put the baby at risk. She was to stay on bed rest for the rest of her pregnancy. She was very weepy at first, but she soon got accustomed to being in bed.

Things started out well, and I was eager to please. I took her meals on a tray and sometimes placed a little flower from the garden next to her plate. She kissed me and told me she loved me. But then things deteriorated, and over the course of the next couple of months, Louise became very sullen and argumentative.

"I don't like eating toast every morning," she said. So, I cooked her some eggs.

"The eggs are too runny."

I was furious. I strode into the room and snatched the eggs away. "Get your own breakfast then," I said.

"You know, the doctor told me to stay in bed."

I felt myself flush with guilt. Louise was right. The doctor had been adamant that she should stay in bed, and I had tried to make her get up.

Then, one day, I was in the kitchen heating some soup and I heard her shout my name.

"What is it, Louise?"

"I want a cup of coffee."

"If you ask nicely, I'll bring you one."

I flopped into a chair, biting my tongue to keep from yelling at her. How could I deal with this petulant wife who had become so demanding? I had to tip-toe around her all the time.

I made two cups of espresso and carried them into the bedroom. She was lying on the bed propped up with pillows and had a very sullen expression on her face. I hardly wanted to sit there and drink coffee with her, but I did.

"You're getting very demanding," I said.

"You know I'm ill."

"You are not ill, Louise. You have high blood pressure, that's all. We are doing everything we can to keep the baby safe."

"I'm stuck here in bed all day and can't get what I want."

"All you have to do is ask nicely." I put my hand on her arm. "You know I'll bring you whatever you need. Be patient. You'll have the baby soon, then you can get out of bed and do what you want."

Louise became more and more demanding. If she wasn't pregnant, I would not have put up with it. Then one night she woke up and found she was lying in a pool of blood. When she saw her blood-soaked nightgown and sheets; she shrieked, "Richard, I'm bleeding."

They rushed Louise to the hospital and took her into a little room. When they examined her, I had to stay outside, and I could hardly bear it. Was she losing our baby? I wished I knew. I paced up and down, wringing my hands. Surely, they could save it. But after some time, the doctor came out of the room and said, "I am so sorry, Monsieur. Your wife has lost the baby." I was so distraught, I cried. I had wanted this baby as much as Louise, and I was terribly sad that she had lost it. Now that little boy would never grow up to be a man and I could never go to his graduation or see him get married.

Louise became impossible after that, and I didn't want to make love to her at all.

"You're being spiteful, Richard," she said. "You won't make love to me because you don't really want a baby."

I thought that was very unreasonable. "Spiteful? Do you know what I'm going through?"

"You're going through?" She said, angrily. "What about me? I can't get pregnant if you don't make love to me, can I?"

"You're grumpy all the time lately. It's very off-putting."

"It's your fault. You don't even try to make love."

Now I was getting really mad, and I clenched my fists. "Don't try! I am trying all I can, but I can't make love to order."

My thoughts were churning round in my head, and I didn't know what to do. My wife had become impossible, and I wanted things to be back the way they were. But I knew that one can never go back in life, so I accepted my fate whatever that would bring.

CHAPTER 38

One day, Louise told me she thought she was pregnant again.

"That's wonderful!" I said. But even though I was overjoyed, I could hardly breathe for fear that this little baby might die as well.

I went to the flower shop on the far side of town and bought Louise the biggest bunch of yellow daisies I could find. Louise loved nothing more than flowers. She had grown many flowers in the garden when she was well, and she loved to arrange them in the house.

I watched her closely after that, peering round the doorway just to make sure she was alright, forbidding her to do anything in the least bit strenuous. But this time she didn't lose the baby, she had the perfect pregnancy, and we had a little girl. She was adorable from the start, with a mass of blonde hair and huge blue eyes. We called her Sophia.

I was over the moon. But Louise lay in bed for hours and put the pillows over her head when Sophia cried. "Pick her up and rock her, will you, Richard?" she said.

"I'm always seeing to her while you sleep," I said, angrily. "I love doing things for the baby, but you're just ignoring her. What's the matter with you?"

"I'm tired."

Then she had me feeding Sophia in the night. She was a very light sleeper and always hungry, so the nights were bad.

"Will you get up and feed her?" Louise said, her voice muffled beneath the pillows.

"I'm always getting up. Why does it have to be me all the time?" I clenched my fists in frustration. "Sophia is your baby, too. She'll begin to think I'm her mother."

Louise buried her head deeper into the pillows. "I'm tired, Richard. Can you see to her?"

Feeling exasperated, I yanked the covers off of her. "You're always tired. That's all you ever say," I shouted at her. "Get up and see to your baby."

Reluctantly, Louise climbed out of bed and fed the baby. But even though I was angry, I could see she was not herself. Her hands shook when she cuddled Sophia in her arms, and she nearly fell asleep when the baby took her bottle. I felt sorry for her, but couldn't think what to do.

Before long, I was feeding Sophia at night while Louise slept. This went on night after night, Louise sleeping through the baby's cries and me giving Sophia her bottle. The baby slept in our room, so I hardly slept at all.

Eventually, I took over, and Louise stayed in bed. When Sophia woke up in the night, I was the one to feed her. I walked up and down the apartment in the middle of the night with her crying on my shoulder. I rubbed her back and sang all the songs I knew, but nothing made her happy. She wanted her mother.

"Sophia is crying for you," I said. "It wouldn't hurt you to get up and see to her."

"I'm too tired," Louise said. Then, instead of talking to me, she pulled the covers over her head again and went back to sleep.

So, life went on, and I took care of Sophia. Of course, this meant I was the one who changed her diapers and gave her baths. Louise was always in bed.

"I can't carry on like this," I finally said to Louise. "Sophia wants her mother."

Louise put her head in her hands and sobbed. "I don't know what's wrong with me," she said. "I don't have any feelings towards her, Richard."

I was feeling sorry for the way I had spoken to her, so I went over and put my arm around her. “What do you mean?”

She looked up through her tears. “I don’t know. I can’t seem to feel any joy in anything.”

I was shocked. That was the first time she had told me she felt like that. She needed to see someone right away.

CHAPTER 39

So, the next day, the three of us went to see her doctor in town. He was a kindly middle-aged man with a mop of curly black hair.

"I've just had a baby and I don't feel well, Doctor," she said. "I can hardly do a thing."

"Have you been sleeping a lot?" he asked.

"Yes, all the time."

"How long has this been going on?"

"Ever since the baby was born."

He picked up his pen and made a note on a pad. "This is quite common," he said. "Some women suffer from depression after having a baby. How do you feel towards the child?"

"I feel totally disconnected from Sophia. I don't want anything to do with her."

He sat back in his chair and looked at Louise. "I think you might have postpartum depression. I'll send you to a psychiatrist to see what she thinks."

She looked horrified. "Surely, I'm not mad, Doctor?"

"You don't have to be mad to see a psychiatrist," he said, smiling. "I think it will be good for you to talk to someone and get some treatment. I could treat you here, but I think it would be best to see a specialist."

They made an appointment for us on the way out and gave Louise a card with the time on it.

I had never heard of post postpartum depression, so I looked it up on the web. There was a lot about it on there, and from reading a couple of articles, I could see that this might be the problem. So, that accounted for Louise's mood. I hadn't realized that she might be ill and pursed my lips with guilt. She must have really been suffering all along.

The next week we kept our appointment. The psychiatrist had gray hair and gold, horn-rimmed glasses. She ushered us into her room and made us feel welcome immediately. She came and sat down beside us. "Tell me what's been happening, Louise?" she said.

"I don't know what's wrong with me, but I haven't been able to feel anything towards Sophia since she was born. I try to love her, but I don't feel connected to her in any way."

"Have you been able to look after her at all?"

"No." She looked up at me, took my hand and smiled. "My

husband has been marvelous about looking after Sophia."

"Let's start you on some medication and see if that makes you feel better."

Louise came home with some medication for her depression, and we read the labels. There were some side effects that we should look out for and tell the doctor if they were bothersome. The more serious side effects were rare, but the medication might take two to six weeks to work, and I couldn't imagine the situation getting any worse.

But I felt quite hopeful now that we had found out the cause of Louise's bad mood. She was ill, and it had nothing to do with me or Sophia. She wanted to be a wonderful mother, but could feel nothing. It made sense and made everything alright. I just hoped she would feel better soon, and I could get some rest.

CHAPTER 40

I was happy to find out the cause of my problems but felt helpless because the tablets took so long to work. I couldn't do anything around the house. Richard was still looking after the baby, and I couldn't see my father in Dijon. I couldn't get word to him either. He must think I was ignoring him. I wanted to take Sophia to see him, but that would have to wait now. And I didn't know if the prison would allow babies in, anyway. When I got better, I would have to ask them if I could bring my baby the next time I saw my father.

I felt so ill and could hardly do a thing. I sat in a chair all day, or sometimes I just stayed in bed. Richard was marvelous, though, and he had such patience with me.

Then, soon after I had taken the pills, I got scared. "Richard," I said one day when he had put Sophia down for her afternoon nap. "I'm feeling a bit strange."

"What's wrong?"

I picked at the bedclothes and couldn't find the words at first. "I'm seeing things in the room."

"What kind of things?"

"Well, I saw a light yesterday. It wasn't like the sun shining in, it was more like a spotlight, very bright and shining directly into my eyes. I tried to block it out, but it was too bright, so I went under the bed covers and waited. When I looked up again, the light was gone."

"You're imagining things. There's nothing in here," he said.

I didn't feel hungry at all, but wanted to eat for Richard's sake. He was going to so much trouble to help me get well. I had never known a man like him before and I really admired him. But we were such a newly married couple, and had married in haste, so we were still learning about each other.

At lunch time, Richard came in with two sandwiches. Sophia was in her crib next to my bed. I looked over at her and saw that she was sleeping. She was a beautiful baby, even when asleep. But I felt nothing for her, nothing! She looked just like a doll lying there. I had never imagined this happening to me. It was too terrible to see my child and not feel anything for her. It made me cry all the time.

CHAPTER 41

I hoped Louise would get better soon, but now she was seeing things in the bedroom. This was a big worry, and I hoped the tablets would be effective soon. Two to six weeks seemed like a very long time to wait. And the doctor had said it might take even longer, which seemed unbearable. I was ready to have my Louise back again. Having a baby had caused her a lot of misery.

But I loved Sophia. She was everything I had ever wanted, and more. I couldn't believe we had such a sweet little daughter. I was so lucky. When Louise got well again, everything would be fine.

I played with my daughter every day and watched her smile. She made me laugh when I bounced her on my knee, and even though things were not working out too well right at that moment, I knew Louise would be better someday. I just hoped it would be soon.

It was so long since Louise had been outside. I thought she could do with getting out of her bed.

"How would you like to take a ride today?" I asked.

"I'm tired, and I want to sleep."

"You've been sleeping for days, and you are missing the beautiful weather outside. The sun is shining, and it's not too cold."

Louise thought for a moment, then said, "Perhaps I would feel better if I went out for a little while." She looked up and smiled.

So, I helped her get out of bed. I put a pink skirt and a white sweater on the bed and waited for her to get dressed. She was such a stylish woman, but now her clothes seemed to hang on her. I knew the depression had that effect, but didn't quite understand how she felt. I had never known anyone with depression, but I could see how sad it made Louise. She often cried for no reason at all.

I had to help her walk because she was so weak from being in bed for days. I put Sophia in her car seat and helped Louise get in the front next to me. She was limp like a doll, and I had to steady her while she stepped into the car and put the seat belt on.

We drove around town and saw people sitting outside the cafes or walking in the cobbled streets. Most of the tourists had left now, and the town was getting back to normal. I saw Mylan and Jacques sitting outside a restaurant and asked Louise if she would like to join them for a cup of coffee.

"No," she said. "I don't want to talk to people just now."

"You don't have to say much, Louise. It might be nice to see some other people for a change."

"No," she said again, more adamantly this time. "I want to stay in the car."

We drove around for a little while, then went straight back home. Louise was so happy to be home that she got into bed with all her clothes on. I made her get up and change into her nightdress. She looked so peaceful in bed, and her cheeks were flushed from the breeze. It got her out of the house, and that could only be a good thing. I had pots and pans to wash, so I went in the kitchen to clear up.

CHAPTER 42

When we got home, I went back to bed. That drive wore me out even though I had done nothing. I pulled up the covers and thought I would get some more sleep. Then I saw something move out of the corner of my eye. It looked like a little animal. A black dog. I looked again, but it was gone. We only had Arlette in the house, and she was white, so I knew it wasn't her.

I lay back on the pillows and closed my eyes, but when I opened them, I saw the black dog again. As soon as I turned my head, it was gone. I thought I might be seeing things that weren't there, and I bit my lip with fright. But I knew I had seen it. There was no question in my mind.

"Richard, come in here!"

He appeared in the doorway with a worried look on his face. "What's the matter?"

"I saw a black dog in here. Can you see it?"

Richard gave the bedroom a cursory glance, then laughed. "There are no animals in here. And Arlette is in the living room, so it can't be her."

"But I saw it."

"You can't have. There's nothing here."

I curled up in bed and shut my eyes, but I couldn't sleep. I knew there was a black dog in my room. I saw it as plain as I saw the baby in her crib.

Richard came in and put Sophia on the changing table. He changed her diapers while I watched and put her in her little pink nightdress. She was so pretty in her nightdress, but I could only look at her dispassionately. I cried because I couldn't feel any love for her at all.

CHAPTER 43

My post-natal appointment came around, but I could not go because I was too ill. Richard called the clinic for me and explained to them what had happened. They asked about the baby and Richard told them he was taking care of Sophia. He said he would be in touch as soon as I felt better.

On Sunday, Richard invited Jean-Claude for lunch. He made a special casserole of beef in red wine. Jean-Claude was in a jolly mood, and he brought me some chocolates. One thing I love is chocolates, but the depression had blunted my taste buds, and I couldn't eat even one of them. I thanked him, of course, and put them to one side. I knew Richard could eat them as he was a chocolate lover like me.

Jean-Claude kissed me on both cheeks. "How are you feeling?"

"I'm so tired all the time," I said.

"Don't you think you should get up and sit at the table? You could even sit outside with a blanket over you. It's not cold today."

I pulled a face at the thought of going outside. "Sitting outside really doesn't appeal to me, Jean-Claude. I'm quite comfortable in here."

There was something I wanted to ask him, but I didn't know how to broach the subject. I thought about it from his point of view, and realized it would make him mad, but I really wanted him to do something for me since I was stuck in bed.

"Will you visit my father?" I asked and looked at him expectantly.

Jean-Claude came right back at me, his face red with rage. "You know what I think of your father, Louise. He's nothing but a murderer, and I won't waste my time visiting him."

"I just wondered, that's all, because I can't get word to him."

"He doesn't deserve such a forgiving daughter as you, Louise. He has done a terrible thing and should suffer his punishment. If that includes not seeing you, then that is only right. He should have thought of the consequences before taking my poor aunt's life."

CHAPTER 44

"Louise asked me to visit her father, Richard," Jean-Claude said when we sat down to eat.

"And will you?"

"Certainly not! That man deserves to rot in prison all by himself. I don't know how on earth she could forgive him for what he's done?"

"Yes, it seems really odd to me. I can't imagine forgiving my father if he had killed my mother. It doesn't bear thinking about."

I ladled out the beef stew onto our plates and took a plate on a tray into Louise's room. She had fallen asleep, and I had to awaken her. Then I went to talk to Jean-Claude.

"I've tried to forgive him, but I just can't let go of the picture I have in my mind of my aunt in pain," he said. "She could never have guessed he was trying to poison her."

"Louise said he sent her away to a mental institution," I said.

"Yes, but she came out just the same as she went in. That's

why he decided to get rid of her, so he gave her the poison. It was drastic, but he was afraid she would attack Louise, he said, so he killed her before something terrible happened."

"Why didn't he divorce her?"

Jean-Claude seemed to be miles away and didn't answer for some time. "Of course, he never expected to be caught, but he was careless and told a friend. The friend reported him to the police."

"That is a very strange story," I said.

I understood Louise better now. She'd lived with a terrible family. She couldn't rely on either her mother or her father for comfort, and now she couldn't relate to her baby. It was all beginning to make sense. The mental illness must be hereditary. I remembered the time she had accused me of having an affair and now she thought she was seeing things. It made me afraid for Sophia. Was she in danger? It was a good thing I was her caretaker, but it made me fear for the future.

CHAPTER 45

The next day, I walked up and down in the apartment, moving things from here to there in an agitated state. Louise was no better, and I didn't know what to do. Perhaps I should call the psychiatrist and see what she thought. I dialed her number. "My wife's not getting any better, Doctor," I said. "She has started seeing things in the room."

"That's serious, *Monsieur*. Bring her in to see me at once."

I frowned, knowing all the while that I couldn't get Louise to leave her room. "She's not able to leave the house just now as she has no energy from the depression. I've tried to get her up, but she won't have it. I am at a loss to know what to do."

"I'll send a prescription to the *pharmacie* and see if that will help. They will take a few days to work. But if she's not better by next week, she will need to go to the hospital."

I hadn't thought that Louise might have to go to the hospital, and I bit my lip in fear. My mind was in a whirl. What would become of her there? It sounded like her mother all over again. I hoped, if she had to go, she wouldn't be gone for long. At least I knew how to look after Sophia, but it was sad that she didn't have a mother to take care of her.

I went immediately to the *pharmacie* and picked up the prescription the psychiatrist had sent.

"Here, darling, take these tablets," I said when I got back. "Let's hope they will make you feel better."

I didn't like to tell her what the psychiatrist had said about her going to the hospital, as I knew she would be terrified since her mother had to stay there for a year. Now I would watch over her even more carefully for the next few days, then call the psychiatrist back if she became worse. I couldn't imagine her having to go to a mental hospital. Tears rushed to my eyes at the thought. She wouldn't be around for Sophia at all if that were to happen. She would miss all the little milestones babies have.

CHAPTER 46

The next evening, I decided Louise was going to get out of bed. She was wasting away as she was. I was concerned for her, but didn't want her to spend any more time in bed than was necessary. She seemed to have given up and had no interest in getting well again.

"Louise, you are going to get up this evening and come and sit with me in the living room."

"You know I can't do that."

"Of course you can. I don't want you to rot away in bed any longer."

So, Louise got out of bed, and I helped her walk to the living room. I hoped it wouldn't be too long before all these medicines made her feel better. She lowered herself into an armchair and I watched her carefully. She was an invalid. I had no idea that depression could make you feel so ill.

I made her a drink of warm tea with honey. She liked tea now and then and I joined her with a cup myself. I thought back over our marriage and marveled at the events that had taken place already. It wasn't so long ago that I had got down on one knee and proposed to her, yet here we were with a baby, and Louise was ill. It all seemed too sudden to me. I had lost track of what my life was like before I met Louise.

I looked over at Sophia, peacefully sleeping, and felt overcome with love for her. I marveled at her tiny little fingers, so perfect, and the way she clenched them, then released them. It was as if she was listening to some mystical music and was capturing the rhythm with her hands.

"It's nice down here in the evening, don't you think?" I said. "It's so peaceful in this apartment, watching the sun go down."

"Yes," she said.

She looked over at the sweet peas I had bought for her and smiled. I wasn't much good at arranging flowers, but I did the best I could. They smelled wonderful in the room. I was pleased she had got up. She needed to get out of bed for a while. I kissed her forehead, then tucked the blanket around her legs.

"It would do you good to get up more often now," I said. "You seem much better here than you do in bed all the time. Sleeping is fine, but you need to live again rather than hibernating and wasting your life away."

She smiled, and I could see that she was trying. It pleased me she'd made the effort to get out of bed. I got her some more tea, and this time I gave her a small chocolate treat to see if she would eat it, but she left it to one side. I couldn't imagine not wanting to eat chocolate, but she had lost her taste for food.

After a while, the sun disappeared behind the wall in the garden, and I put on the lamps in the corners of the room. I could see Louise was tired, so I helped her get into bed.

CHAPTER 47

As soon as I got back into bed, I fell asleep. Then I heard someone calling my name. "Louise, Louise." I jumped out of my sleep and called out, "What do you want, Richard?"

He appeared at the bedroom door, a worried look on his face. "I didn't call you," he said. "You must have been dreaming."

So, that was it. I had been dreaming and heard my name called. It gave me a shiver down my back. It had seemed so real, like Richard's voice calling me out of my sleep. Then I remembered the black dog and the spotlight and started to cry. "I'm afraid, Richard. I don't know what to do."

"What do you mean? You know I'm there in the next room and can come any time you need me."

I felt queasy inside and wondered what was happening to me. Was I just imagining the things in my room? But I was certain I saw them. I felt sure they were there. And I could definitely hear the voice calling to me. I had no explanation for it.

Richard went back into the living room, and I must have dozed off. But suddenly I was awake again, bathed in sweat. Did I have a fever? Perhaps that was the reason I was seeing and hearing things. I put my hand to my forehead and felt the beads of sweat accumulating there. My back was stuck to my nightdress.

"Richard," I called out. "Would you come here and bring the thermometer with you? I think I have a fever."

Richard took my temperature, and it was normal, so there was no fever. I had just been upset by the voice that called my name. I felt my tears well up again because I had never felt so ill in all my life. The depression was draining me, and I wished the tablets would work soon, then maybe I could get some peace.

CHAPTER 48

The next day, I thought I had to get out of the house, so went for a walk with Sophia in her stroller. I felt guilty leaving Louise in bed but knew she would be alright, and Sophia and I needed the fresh air.

I love winter in Cannes. The tourists had all gone home and the little cafes were full of locals. My favorite cafe was half way down *la Croisette*, so I walked straight there with Sophia. Mylan and Jacques were sitting in the corner. I walked over and joined them at their table.

When my coffee came, it smelled delicious, and I watched the foam on the top disappear when I stirred it around in the cup. I smiled and sat back in my chair. It was so nice to relax and not to be worried about Louise all the time. The events of the past few weeks had completely drained me, and I had quite forgotten how wonderful it felt to be out of the house.

Jacques took to Sophia immediately. “Can I hold her?” he said.

“I don’t think she’ll go to a stranger.”

So Jacques stroked her cheek instead. “Sophia. My precious.”

She smiled up at him.

I put the back of the stroller down and rocked the baby until she went to sleep. Quite a few people I knew were in the cafe and I waved at some of them. It made me feel like a different person from the one who had been taking care of Louise and the baby for so long.

"Haven't seen you around for quite a while," Mylan said.

I suddenly felt at a loss for words. I wanted to tell them about Louise's illness, but wondered how that might sound to someone else. Maybe they had never dealt with depression. It was impossible to explain how Louise said it made her feel.

I sighed. "Louise has been very ill."

They both looked concerned. "What's wrong with her?" Jacques said.

"The doctor says she's depressed. I've been very worried about her."

"You should have rung," Mylan said. "I could have come round and been company for you."

I was pleased he said that as I could have done with the company. It was remiss of me not to ask. But I couldn't imagine what they would think of Louise. She had changed so much, they wouldn't recognize her.

CHAPTER 49

While Richard was out, I tried to think clearly about my future, but my mind was so fuzzy I couldn't really come to any conclusions. Being ill like that was not something I had been used to, as I had always been a very healthy woman. Instead, I had been in bed for weeks and hadn't even cared much about Richard or Sophia. It worried me I couldn't care for Sophia like I should, and I thought about what it would be like when she was older. She would be bonded with Richard by then and probably think of me as a stranger. It was a very frightening thought.

"Louise," the familiar voice suddenly called to me. "Louise, you must get up now."

I gasped. I knew Richard was out, so it couldn't be him calling to me. Who was it? The male voice was coming from somewhere, but I couldn't tell where. Was it in my head?

"Louise, get up," the voice said firmly, and I immediately sat up and slipped out of bed. I put on my robe over my nightdress, slid my feet into my slippers, and slowly made my way into the dining room. The house was empty and felt strange without Richard and the baby there. The floor seemed to be at an angle, and I couldn't walk straight. Was the floor slanted, I wondered? Looking down, I saw nothing, but it felt weird. I thought I would fall off the floor. The world spun around and around inside my head as I hung onto the dining chair. I couldn't tell whether I was standing still or lying down.

Then I noticed something odd. What once was a chair now looked all crooked and bent out of shape. I watched as the other chairs bent and became a brilliant shade of orange. I was standing in the middle of a mass of orange-colored furniture.

Then there was the noise. I didn't recognize it at first, but then I realized it was a choir singing. Hundreds of female voices were singing loudly inside my head. I listened intently.

I gripped the back of the chair and wished, more than anything, that Richard was there. I remembered he had gone for a walk with Sophia, but I couldn't remember what time he'd left.

"Louise, go into the kitchen," the voice said above the choir, and I followed the commands. Arlette was in her box, scratching at the litter when I went into the kitchen. She turned her back to me.

"Now look up high in the cabinet above the sink and see what you can find."

I carefully stood on a stool and looked in the cabinet like the voice demanded. My world was spinning around in my head, so I had to hold on to the cabinet door to steady myself.

“Look for the rat poison, Louise.”

I searched in the cabinet and found all kinds of things up there —— cans of peas, carrots, soup, apple pie filling and more. I hadn’t cleared that cupboard out in all the time I had lived in Richard’s apartment. And since he kept things for years, who knew what I might find? I moved the bottles and cans to one side, and right at the back, I found a container of rat poison. It was so old the top was rusty, and I could hardly read the label. I got down off the stool with the rat poison in my hand.

“Unscrew the jar, Louise.”

I held the jar tightly in one hand and tried to unscrew the lid, but it wouldn’t budge, so I had to use a knife.

“Now take down two glasses,” the voice said, “and make you and Richard some drinks.”

Richard liked orange juice, and I found some in the fridge. I took a spoon and measured out an ounce or two of the powder and put it in one of the tall glasses of orange juice. It was cloudy at first, then it dissolved into the juice. I filled the other glass with orange juice, then I put the rat poison back in the cabinet over the sink.

"Richard must die," the voice said, and I looked up, startled. Where was this voice coming from?

I took a glass of juice and went back into the living room with its mass of orange chairs, and waited for Richard to come back with the baby. It was quite warm in the house, but I was shivering. I put a throw around my shoulders, but I still felt cold inside. I drank the juice and put down the glass.

Hours passed by and Richard didn't come home. I passed the time by looking through some of his books. They were all about architecture and history, which didn't interest me at all. I glanced at the pile of newspapers he kept in the corner of the room. I had tried to get him to throw them away, but he wouldn't hear of it. Then I heard the key turn in the lock and my breath came quickly. Richard was home.

"Hello, Louise." Richard called out above the din in my ears, but it didn't sound like Richard at all. I thought it must be a stranger that had entered the apartment, and I cringed in fear.

"Kill him now. Kill Richard," said the voice in an urgent tone.

So, I went into the kitchen and said hello. It was Richard, after all, not a stranger. I picked up the other glass of orange juice and gave it to him to drink.

"Oh, I'm so glad you're up," Richard said, and it seemed like the words echoed their way back to me and drowned out the choir for a moment. "I had such a good time visiting with my friends in the cafe. They asked how you were."

The choir was singing loudly now, and I could hardly hear what he said. Richard drank the orange juice straight down and thanked me for getting it for him. He put his glass down on the counter. I watched him intently to see what would happen next.

We went back into the dining room with its mass of orange chairs. He was talking to me about something, but I couldn't hear him above the choir. The dining chair he was sitting on turned a beautiful shade of green. It bent double under his weight.

I watched him closely, waiting for some sign that the poison was working, but he seemed the same as always. I didn't know what I was expecting. Perhaps it took a while for the rat poison to work.

Then I began feeling very dizzy and had to hang onto the arm of the chair as it spun around the room. I thought I was going to be sick, but the waves washed over me. I stayed still and listened to the choir singing.

"Louise," said Richard, jumping up and coming towards me.

I shrunk back in the chair. "No, no, no!" I shouted at him, but he came nearer and put his arm around my shaking shoulders.

I felt really strange now and could hardly breathe. My stomach was hurting like never before. I put my hand on it and felt lumps under my skin. Was it my imagination, or were there really lumps there? No, I was certain I could feel them.

I turned around in the chair and vomited orange fluid all over the floor.

"What's the matter, matter, matter with you, Louise, Louise, Louise?"

My stomach hurt really badly now, and I cried out. The lumps were growing larger under my hand. Was I imagining them? My eyes were hurting, and everything was too bright. I could hardly see. The choir was singing louder and louder inside my head.

"I'm going to call the ambulance," Richard said.

Now, pain wracked my body, and I squirmed around in the chair. The pain was terrible, and I felt my head spinning and my hands shaking. Perhaps I should get back to bed. I tried to get up from the chair, but collapsed on the floor instead.

CHAPTER 50

I tried to get Louise up on the chair, but I couldn't manage it because she was twisting and turning in my arms. I called the ambulance right away, and the paramedics rushed in and looked at her. They took her temperature and her blood pressure and felt her clammy skin. "Do you know what's wrong with her?" one asked.

"I've got no idea," I said. "She was fine when I went out, but I came back and found her like this."

"We've got to get her to the hospital immediately."

They put her on a stretcher and carried her out to the ambulance. I picked up Sophia and held her in my arms. She was too tiny to know what was happening, of course, and I was glad. I put Sophia in the car seat and followed the ambulance into town. I couldn't imagine what had happened while I was gone. Louise was in bed when I left. But something had made her get up and go into the dining room without my help. I wondered what possessed her.

I ran into a storm on the way to the hospital. My windshield wipers could hardly keep up. I saw lightning in the distance and thunder boomed all around me. My eyes grew tired trying to peer through the windshield and Sophia started crying, but I couldn't stop now. I wanted to get to the hospital to see what had happened to Louise.

When I got there, I followed the ambulance to the emergency room. I put Sophia in her stroller and went inside. Like all hospitals, it was like a beehive, with people rushing about everywhere. The florescent lights were so bright they hurt my eyes. There were a few people in the waiting room, and Sophia and I joined them. Beads of sweat formed on my brow, and I was terrified. Something had gone badly wrong while I was out. What had happened to Louise?

I waited for what seemed like an eternity. Doctors and nurses came and went, and a young couple with their child entered the waiting room. They were talking between them, but I couldn't make out what they were saying. It seemed like an interminable wait. I thought we had been forgotten, so I went out into the corridor and spoke to a nurse at the desk.

"We're working on her now, *Monsieur*," she told me, and I went back and sat down.

A few minutes later, a doctor with white hair in a white coat appeared in the doorway. He ushered us out of the waiting room and took us to his office. "I'm sorry to tell you, *Monsieur*, but Louise has slipped into a coma, so we shall have to wait for her to recover."

"How long will that take?" I asked, then realized that was a stupid question.

The doctor looked at me intently and smiled. "Unfortunately, we cannot predict such a thing. But you can be sure she will be taken good care of."

"Do you know what's wrong with her?"

"Not at the moment. We're still carrying out tests."

CHAPTER 51

When he left, I took Sophia out of the hospital and went for a walk in the park across the road. The storm had left huge puddles on the footpath, and the wind was so strong I could barely stand up. I wanted to have time to think before going back to the hospital. Leaning forward, I drew Sophia's blanket higher around her face, and I pulled my collar up to my ears. I sat down on a park bench out of the wind and pushed Sophia back and forth in her stroller.

Very few people were out on this blustery day. Most of them must have been sensible and stayed at home. But there was a young couple kissing on a bench, and it reminded me of how Louise and I had been not so long ago. It made my heart ache. What had happened to my beautiful butterfly?

I bit my lip and felt the tears welling up in my eyes. I shouldn't have left her when she was so ill. It was thoughtless of me. And now, look at her. When would she wake up and talk to me? I wiped away the tears, then I walked back to the hospital with Sophia.

The nurse allowed me to see Louise, and I went with Sophia to her room. I felt quite hopeless. Sophia was gurgling and had no idea what was going on. Poor Louise was lying on her back with her eyes closed. She was hooked up to several machines, some of them beeping, but I didn't know what they were all for.

"Wake up now, darling," I whispered in her ear, but of course, there was no reply. I sat down beside the bed and put Sophia on my lap. She was so young, so innocent. Her hands were a little chilled, so I put her mittens on. I sat with Louise for a little while, then I kissed her cheek and went back to the car. I strapped Sophia in her car seat and put the stroller in the trunk. Then we drove home.

I had a call from the hospital later that day. "We have some blood test results on your wife, *Monsieur*, and we would like you to come to the hospital to talk to the doctor."

When Sophia and I got back to the hospital, I put her in her stroller. We were shown into the doctor's office again. It was the same doctor who I had seen earlier that day and he ushered me to sit down.

"I shall get straight to the point, *Monsieur*," he said. "We found thallium in your wife's blood and urine. That's what has caused her illness."

Suddenly, the whole story of how Louise's father had poisoned her mother with thallium came back to me. My mouth dropped open in horror.

"Did you know your wife was suicidal?"

"No, I had no idea. I wouldn't have left her alone if I'd known."

"We shall have to call the police, *Monsieur*. We need to discover if this was a suicide or ..."

"Louise wouldn't have wanted to kill herself," I said. "She had everything to live for." But all the while I was talking, I wondered if people were now thinking that I had tried to kill my wife. It was a nightmare being acted out in broad daylight.

CHAPTER 52

Two plain-clothed detectives came into the room, and handcuffs clicked shut on my wrists. A woman police officer took Sophia away from me in her stroller. "We are arresting you for the attempted murder of Louise Baker. You will come with us down to the station."

"No, no, you don't understand." I tried to protest, but they whisked me away in a police car. The seat was made of ice-cold metal, and I was very uncomfortable sitting in the back as the car swept through the traffic. I was glad they didn't put the sirens on because I didn't want other people to see me. Once, when we stopped at traffic lights, two people in a car looked in at me. I gave them a piercing look, then we drove off again.

When we got to the station, they booked me, put me in a cold, windowless room, and left me to wait. There was a table and four chairs, but nothing else in the room. Two detectives finally came in and sat down. One started writing something down on his notepad. "Would you like representation?" he asked me.

I was indignant. "I've done nothing wrong, so why would I

want a lawyer?"

He duly noted that on his pad.

"Where have they taken my baby?" I demanded.

"She will be safe with the woman detective, *Monsieur.*"

They questioned me for the next three hours, and I told them everything I knew. I had gone out for a walk and met up with some friends, then when I returned, I found Louise on the floor writhing in agony. They wanted to know the names of my friends, so I told them. I knew Mylan and Jacques would vouch for me.

I tried to look calm, but I was feeling anything but calm inside. I felt the blood rush to my face and wrung my hands under the table.

Then, against my protests, they put me in a cell. The door clunked shut behind them. Nothing like that had ever happened to me before, and I bit my lip in fear. I was told I could make one call, so I called Jean-Claude. He came straight away, and I told him what had happened to Louise.

He hung his head and sighed. "I was afraid of this. Louise is living her past all over again. She is sick like her mother."

"I thought she was getting better," I said. "She got herself out of bed and must have gone into the kitchen for something when I was out. I found the stool out of place and the cupboard door above the sink was slightly open."

Then I realized that I'd left some rat poison in the cupboard. Why hadn't I thrown it away? It must have been there for years. So, I was to blame. I'd been instrumental in causing Louise's illness.

Just then, a detective unlocked the cell door and came inside. "I'm sorry to have to tell you, *Monsieur*, but your wife has succumbed to the poison. She passed away in the hospital just now."

My mouth dropped open, but I couldn't utter a sound. No words came out when I tried to speak. I looked towards Jean-Claude and saw the tears well up in his eyes. He looked deathly ill. The policeman said my charge had now been upgraded to murder. I couldn't believe all this was happening. It was too much to take in. I tried to go over it in my mind. My wife was dead, and I was being charged with her murder. What was I to do now?

I thought about the poisoning and wondered how Louise had done it. She must have climbed up on the stool and found the rat poison over the sink. Then I remembered the glass of orange juice she had made for me. With horror, I realized she had probably wanted me to drink the poison. What on earth possessed her to do such a wicked thing? But I knew exactly what it was, as it was her father's ploy. She was the daughter of a murderer, after all. Louise was ill, and I had almost died.

I was interviewed again later that day as the police wanted to confirm where I had been that morning. I told them I was with Mylan and Jacques at the restaurant. Certainly they could vouch for me. I said I loved my wife and would never do anything to harm her. But I didn't think they believed me. Later I was let out on bail because they deemed I wasn't a danger to the public. I picked up Sophia and went home.

It was wonderful to be let out of the police cell, but I had to go home to an empty apartment. Now I was without a wife and poor Sophia was without a mother. It was so terrible I couldn't think about it just then.

Sitting at the kitchen table, I realized the police had taken the two glasses away as evidence. I walked around the empty apartment in a daze and went into the bedroom. I saw where Louise had left the bed unmade when she got up. It was like a bad dream. When would I wake up?

CHAPTER 53

Two days later, the phone rang. It was the police, and they wanted to see me down at the station. When I got there, they said, "You are exonerated, *Monsieur*. We only found Louise's fingerprints on the glass and your friends could vouch for you at the time of the incident. Thallium takes a few hours to work. Louise drank the poison while you were out."

I felt faint and heaved a sigh of relief. It was terrible that Louise was dead, but at least I was not going to prison for her murder.

"Your wife was not well. We cleared it with the psychiatrist, who said she was having an episode of psychosis at the time she tried to kill herself."

Sadly, the fact they had ruled it as a suicide didn't make me feel any better. I had lost my wife and had a baby to bring up on my own. It was a cruel twist of fate.

I would have told them she was trying to kill me like her father had done, but I thought better of it. That would complicate things too much. It was unnecessary information.

I drove down *la Croisette* and took a walk with Sophia down to the beach. We sat down on the sand and watched the waves coming in and going out. I finally broke down and sobbed uncontrollably. Tears ran down my cheeks and wouldn't stop. My poor Louise. My love. Something had possessed her to do such a terrible thing. She wasn't in her right mind at all. I was sure she didn't want either one of us to die. It had all been a horrible mistake.

I tried imagining what was going through Louise's mind. Had she been psychotic at the time? Was that why she did it? Her mother had a mental illness, so it must have been genetic. It wasn't her fault. If she was mentally ill, I could begin to understand it now.

I took Sophia out of her stroller and rocked her on my knee. She was smiling, completely unaware of what had happened to her mother. I leaned forward and kissed the top of her head and brushed a strand of her blonde hair away from her face. Nothing more could be done. Louise had met her fate, and I would have to bring up Sophia on my own. I put her back in her stroller, walked back to the car, and drove home.

The clock struck the hour when we walked in through the front door. I took Sophia out of her stroller and put her back in her crib. She was hungry now, so I measured out some formula and fed her. Sophia was such a good baby. She hardly ever cried. I looked into her deep blue eyes and wondered what she was thinking. What would become of her now that her mother was dead? Would she want to know the story of her mother's poisoning and her grandfather's incarceration at some time in the future? I bit my lip and shuddered. I would have to see to that when the time came.

Jean-Claude came round later that day, and we held each other tightly. He had lost his cousin, and I had lost my wife. Sophia had lost her mother.

"I will help you bring up Sophia," Jean-Claude said. "I will always be there for you if you need me."

"I know you will," I said. "You have been a good friend."

I thought back to when I had met Louise. It wasn't so long ago, but so much had happened since then. When I closed my eyes, I could still see her sitting there reading something on her Kindle in Jean-Claude's house. It was an ill-fated meeting. But I could never have guessed what was to follow. Perhaps I should have heeded Jean-Claude's warnings, but then I would never have had my Sophia. I looked at her in her crib and knew everything would be alright.

www.ingramcontent.com/pod-product-compliance
Ingram Content Group UK Ltd.
Pitfield, Milton Keynes, MK11 3LW, UK
UKHW040022200726
13854UKWH00001B/300

9 798869 217530